TRIPLE THREAT

A Tale of Friendship, Love, and Betrayal

JASON B. RASH

SONCOAST
PUBLISHING

Hey Jenny,

I Am so proud of
your pickleball
progress.
enjoy the book.

Jason

Triple Threat

Copyright © 2021 by Jason B. Rash

First printing May, 2021

ISBN 978-1-953406-15-6 Paperback

ISBN 978-1-953406-16-3 Ebook

Scripture taken from the New King James Version®. Copyright © 1982 by Thomas Nelson. Used by permission. All rights reserved.

Cover design by Abigail Jackson

Book design by Martine Bates Fairbanks

Published by Soncoast Publishing

P.O. Box 1503

Hartselle, AL 35640

www.soncoastpublishing.com

PREFACE

"Nothing in all Nature is more certain than the fact that no single thing or event can stand alone. It is attached to all that has gone before it, and it will remain attached to all that will follow it. It was born of some cause, and so it must be followed by some effect in an endless chain."

—American surgeon and author Julian P. Johnson (1873–1939)

CHAPTER ONE

Saturday, 9:00 a.m., August 18 — Week 36

*W*ell, it is that time of year when some kids are excited and others are nervous. I'm so tired of being the nervous one. Monday morning I will start a new school—again. I think this is number six in the last four years. It all seems like a blur to tell the truth.

I've been practicing my handshake and "nice-to-meet-you" face all week. "Hello, I'm Christine, I mean Chris, I go by Chris," I say. "It's nice to meet you."

"The pleasure is all mine," they say. Yeah right. If only it would go that smoothly. Not too many people care about the new girl. Sure, if I were gorgeous or a super athlete or a super anything they probably would, but I'm not. And I'm okay with that, I think. I just need something good in my life.

I know I make it difficult on people. I'm not the easiest person to approach, and I get really nervous around people. The truth is I'm usually just distracted. I'm sad, and it is something that is hard to hide. My mind always goes back to Mom and Dad. I miss them so much, especially this time of year.

They were great parents. No matter how rough my day was or how busy life got, they always were there for me. What I loved the most was the way they supported whatever I was interested in at the time. They never missed anything—piano recitals or soccer games. They were there. And whether it was a win or a loss, they loved me so much. To this day, I still can't see a commercial about drunk driving without becoming angry. That driver took the most precious people in the world away from me.

Mom was always the best when it came to giving me a big sendoff for my first day of school. Of course, Aunt Kathy does a good job also. I am lucky to have such a cool aunt. She gave up a lot for me, and she even almost died for me. I mean literally. You see, I had been living with my Aunt Kathy and Uncle Steve for almost four years when Kathy discovered that Steve had been sexually abusing me. When she stepped in to protect me, he hurt her. She ended up in the hospital for days.

Once she healed and got the full story about what he was doing to me as well as the harsh mental abuse that went along with it, we packed up and headed as far away from him as we could possibly get. Since then, jobs have been hard to come by, but Kathy takes care of me and does her best to provide for me. Kathy and I have been on our own now for almost two years, and she loves me like I am her own. She is what I would call a free spirit. She is dating again, and I'm not so sure about this guy either, but we will see.

How did I get off on that anyway? I have my own problems to worry about and need to focus on me for now. School Monday morning! This time around it's going to be awesome because this time I'm a senior, and I am going to rule the school. Ha! … It's 10:00 a.m. Until next week.

～

TRIPLE THREAT

Saturday, 9:00 a.m., August 25 — Week 37

I did it! I survived the first week of school at Heights Central. It wasn't as bad as I thought it was going to be. I went through my usual routine of trying to figure out who everyone is and where they fall on the social scale. It was your usual collection of groups — athletes, skateboarders, chess club, band members, and cheerleaders.

I love to watch the other students and try to figure them out. Most people just kind of blend in with their groups but there were two guys who really stood out among the crowd: Alex Maddox, the quarterback of the Heights Central Bears football team, and Trevor Williams, his goofy sidekick and fellow teammate. They were always cutting up and laughing. Everyone seemed to be at ease around them. They were at the top of the social ladder but they didn't seem to look down on others. This was a refreshing change from what I have experienced at my other schools.

On the girls' side, everyone kept calling this obvious trio of standouts "Triple Threat." They were beautiful, smart, and popular. Michelle Gadsden was best friend to the top dog Laura Stewart, and then the third one was Crystal somebody. They all three are super confident and not afraid of anything. They don't seem open to making new friends or inviting outsiders into their group. In fact, they don't seem to have too much interest for anyone besides themselves — except for Alex and Trevor, that is. I watched several people try to get in with their little group during the first week of school, only to be humiliated in front of everyone. Funny enough though, those people will try again. I guess they are just gluttons for punishment. I wonder what it would be like to be one of those girls. A girl who can have the boy everyone wants. A girl who fears nothing. Maybe someday I'll know, but for now I'll just have to settle for being plain old Chris.

It's 10:00 a.m. Until next week.

~

Saturday, 9:00 a.m., September 1 — Week 38

This week I continued to learn more about the social culture around school. I found myself almost in a stalker-type mode when it came to Alex. I'm not talking fatal attraction or anything that drastic, but it would be nice to get to know him. I know it is a long shot and probably ridiculous that he would ever pay attention to someone like me, but it is still fun to dream about. From what I can tell, he is super kind to everyone, and Trevor is kind as well. Trevor is so silly, and you can tell Alex loves to laugh at his jokes. Trevor is a little rough around the edges, but Alex has a tenderness about him. You can just tell he has a good heart.

As I was watching Alex from a distance on Tuesday, I saw Laura come up and give him a kiss. They are dating. They are a power couple. No, they are THE Power Couple and apparently quite serious from what I have observed. The discovery of Alex having such a beautiful girlfriend had me quite depressed, but then something amazing happened. I caught a break. Being the klutz that I am, I dropped my books in the hall and — call it luck or call it fate — Alex was right there to help me pick them up.

"I think we have algebra together," he said. It felt like time was standing still.

I fumbled for some clever comeback that would make a first impression that nobody would ever forget but all I could manage to say was a shaky, "Yes." Or I might have said, "Uh huh." I can't remember. He asked me if I was any good at the subject and then I started to relax a little. I told him it was my favorite. I was worried I sounded like a nerd but I could tell he didn't think that at all. He told me it was one of his worst subjects and he was wondering if I would be interested in helping him. I said I would love to help him, realizing that sounded a bit strange. I backpedaled and said, "I mean I would be glad to help you."

He smiled and said, "My name is Alex." And I got to use the opening phrase I had practiced so much before the first day of school.

"Hello, I'm Christine. I go by Chris. It's nice to meet you."

Alex said something about seeing me in algebra and figuring out when we could study together, but I couldn't concentrate on his words. All I could think about was how such a dreamy guy could be so kind and that he was talking to me — the new girl — the girl other students never noticed or cared about. My eyes were locked on his and my smile was probably pretty goofy. I'm not even sure what I said as he walked away.

Mom always said that being good at math was important. I never really understood why, but now it is finally going to pay off. I am so excited. I can't wait for our first study session.

It's 10:00 a.m. Until next week.

CHAPTER TWO

Saturday, 9:00 a.m., September 8 — Week 39

I started helping Alex study this week, and we ended up spending a lot of time together. What was supposed to be a one-night study session Tuesday turned into us meeting at lunch on Wednesday and Friday to go over problems. He also met me at the local library Thursday afternoon after practice. He is already learning how to do the problems and understand them, and it is exciting for him. I feel like we are developing a friendship as well. I have really enjoyed my time with him and learning some of the little things about him.

I love the relationship he has with his parents and the way he carries the key ring his mom gave him as a reminder to always try to do the right thing and stay out of trouble. It has some type of reference on it, Luke 8:17, I think. I'm not really sure I fully understand it, but I can tell it means a lot to him.

Alex is so amazing. He seems to have it all together.

Math is the only thing he seems to struggle with, and he can't afford to be on any kind of academic probation because the football team cannot afford to lose their star, nor can he afford to lose possible scholarship opportunities.

Another interesting thing happened this week and her name is Laura. She approached me and asked if I have been having fun with her boyfriend. She did not appreciate all the time he was putting into studying already, so now she is really frustrated because he started spending time with me, too. I assured her that all we are doing is studying and that he is making great progress and that I am proud of him. I thought that was a kind thing to say but she laughed at me. "Why else would someone like Alex be hanging out with someone like you?" Laura spewed.

For a moment, her words hurt me. Could Alex be using me? Surely not. He truly seems to appreciate my help, and he does talk to me about other things as well. He really is a great guy. I mean, he didn't have to compliment my dress Wednesday on picture day, but he did, and that made me feel good. Of course, later that day Laura told me my dress was outdated and boring. She said she can't figure out how Alex can even stand to be around me with the way I look.

Laura, Michelle, and Crystal surrounded my locker later that same day and told me my hair, clothes, and eyes were all droopy. And before I knew it, they were all three laughing and calling me Droopy. "I think we just found the perfect name for our new friend here," Laura said.

I closed my locker and got out of there, almost tripping as I hurried away. But it didn't stop. Triple Threat was able to make this my official nickname by the end of the week, and everyone laughs when they say it. Most of these kids don't even know me. I tried not to let it get to me, but I cried myself to sleep last night.

My first thought this morning was to tell Alex on Monday so he could help me, but then I remembered how Laura warned me about saying anything to Alex. She assured me it can get a whole lot worse and not to push her. Can they really be more cruel? If I'm such a boring, ugly, outdated nobody with a nickname like Droopy, then why do they feel the need to hurt me? It doesn't make sense.

It's 10:00 a.m. Until next week.

～

Saturday, 9:00 a.m., September 15 — Week 40

This week, Alex insisted that I come to the football game on Friday night. He said it would be a lot of fun and that I was a big part of the team. I asked him what he was talking about, and he explained to me that he had told the coach, his teachers, and Laura that without my help he probably would not even be playing. "Avoiding defensive linemen was one thing, but trying to avoid equations was impossible," he joked. "I would have never made it this far without you."

Alex thanked me and gave me a big hug, a hug I wished would have never ended. But just as I was starting to daydream with his arms wrapped around me, he shook me and said that he still needed my help, that I wasn't off the hook from tutoring. I laughed and agreed, breathing a sigh of relief because I definitely wasn't ready for our study sessions to be over.

Alex could tell I seemed anxious and asked me if something was on my mind, so I decided to try to talk to him. I started by asking him if he considered us friends. He just rolled his eyes, called me "silly," and gave me another bear hug. "Of course, we are," he said as I saw Laura from the corner of my eye looking at me with what I could only describe as a death threat. When Alex backed away and saw my face, he asked me if everything was okay. I fumbled for the words, "I'm fine." He didn't push, but he did make a reference to how pale I looked and was concerned that I wasn't telling him the truth. I thought that was sweet. I settled myself, insisted I was okay, and said I needed to get going. I didn't dare tell him about Triple Threat since the girls, and especially Laura, had threatened me with nothing short of my life.

"What about the game?" he yelled to me as I hurried off. "I'll think about it," I said over my shoulder, avoiding any eye contact with Laura or Triple Threat.

I made it through the week with only a few snarly comments from the girls and a couple more evil glances — that is, until the game Friday night. I decided to go and loved every second of watching Alex play. He even waved to me. That infuriated Laura because she seems to know every move he is making when it comes to me. I was tucked away at the top of the bleachers, hiding from the world, but she still found me.

After the game, Triple Threat approached me and was driving me into a corner. I was doing my best to escape without looking or talking to them, but they would not let me pass. When they finally had me cornered, Laura asked if I enjoyed the game from the losers' section. I asked them to please leave me alone and let me pass.

"You think you can spend all the time you want with my boyfriend, take him away from me, and just get to walk away?" Laura responded. "I don't think so, Droopy. Alex is using you and he is too kind to say anything, but you make him sick. If he didn't need to pass that class so badly, he would never even give you a second thought."

I tried so hard not to give in to my emotions because I didn't want Laura to win, but I couldn't stop the tears. "Now there's the droopy face I love to see," Laura said as she started a cheer to entertain the crowd of students gathering around to watch the encounter. "Give me a 'D.' Give me an 'R.'" And on they went to spell out "Droopy" while laughing and pointing at me.

The crowd began to suffocate me, and my crying became more intense. Why would no one help me? It was as if the whole world had me cornered and everyone was making fun of me.

About that time, Alex came out of the locker room and saw what was going on. "Enough! Get out of here," he said. He almost got into a fight with one of the students who continued, and he and Laura exchanged a few heated words. She was really angry with him.

I, however, almost jumped into his arms. Alex was my hero. He had rescued me and walked me out of the crowd and to my car. He gave me a hug and said he was sorry as he opened my car door. If only I could have just thanked him and driven away, but no, not me. I have to go and do something stupid. I tried to give him a kiss. Arghhhhh! What's wrong with me? I've ruined everything.

Alex pushed me away the second I leaned in. "What are you doing, Chris?"

I dropped my head in shame. "Could you not love someone like me?" I asked him. "We are friends but that's all," Alex said. "I'm with Laura. I love Laura."

"How could you love someone that mean and ugly?" I asked.

"She's not mean and ugly," he replied. "She is just struggling with some things right now. I'm sorry she has been so cruel to you lately. She is usually a nice person, but she is struggling with jealousy right now. She doesn't like the fact that I need your help so much and how much I rely on you."

It's 10:00 a.m. Until next week.

~

Saturday, 9:00 a.m., September 22 — Week 41 — Homecoming

This week was one of the toughest I have faced in a while. Aunt Kathy was really concerned about me, but I just couldn't explain to her all that was going on. I really needed my mom. This week marked the three-year anniversary of when Steve first raped me. It is something that I can't explain. I don't know if I will ever heal completely from that nightmare.

And, of course, Triple Threat continues their attacks. They are relentless, but I manage to survive somehow.

It was homecoming week and, as much as I wanted to feel and be part of the festivities, I just don't fit in. Still, Alex — my weakness and my one strength — insisted that I go to the homecoming game and even the dance. I told him all week long that I just really didn't think it was a good idea. I wish I had listened to my instincts.

The thought of having the opportunity to dance with Alex, no matter how small the chance, was so compelling that it drew me in. I even had it all worked out in my mind days before the dance.

There I am standing all alone in the corner waiting for my hero to ask me to dance. He approaches the DJ and asks him to play "I Don't Want to Miss a Thing" by Aerosmith, and then walking past everyone else he comes to me and asks in the most charming of voices, "My lady, may I have this dance?"

I say, "Certainly. I never deny a man as handsome as yourself a dance."

Of course, what really happened was nothing like my dream. In fact, the whole weekend turned into a nightmare. It all started with a card I made Alex wishing him good luck in the game. I put it in his Algebra book on Thursday when we finished studying. He didn't mention it Friday at school so I was afraid I had made him uncomfortable. It wasn't until right before the game that my mind was put at ease. Alex looked up into the stands and waved to me again. I knew then everything was all right. *I might just get that dance*, I thought, and perked up even though I still have to sit by myself at the game. No one ever invited me to sit with them, but I was used to it. Plus, we won the game and everyone was in crazy celebration mode, so I cheered along with everyone else.

The dance was pretty much what I expected. The popular kids were on the dance floor and the more insecure kids were hanging out drinking punch. And then there were a few loners like me. It took about an hour for the football players to begin to arrive, but still no Alex and it was now around 10:30. I thought I might actually make it without a Triple Threat attack during the dance, but no sooner did I actually think it than I turned around to see Laura, Michelle, and Crystal walk up to me carrying the card I had made for Alex. And, of course, as if right on cue the DJ began to play "Hit Me Baby One More Time" by Britney Spears.

Laura had written a bunch of words and statements that were not part of the kind and encouraging card I had written to Alex. They made it seem like I was some kind of crazy, obsessed girl who had no sense of reality. The stuff they wrote was mean and embellished. As they read it aloud, the other students couldn't help but laugh and point at me.

"I love you, Alex. You are the man of my dreams," Laura said in a wimpy, whiny voice. "No one will ever compare to you."

"I didn't write those things," I protested.

"I think you did," Laura retorted. "But let's not leave out the best parts," she continued. By now a large crowd had gathered around and that all-too-familiar feeling of being trapped was happening again. "Hey, everyone," said Laura. "Droopy here is in love with my boyfriend."

It was a struggle, but I finally broke free of the group and ran out of the gym crying — and ran right into Alex. He almost lost his footing, stumbling a bit before realizing it was me. He was annoyed and even impatient with me as I tried to apologize and explain. He was still pumped from the game and kept talking about how it was going to be a special night and he was ready to get to the dance. This was the first time I had seen such selfishness in Alex, and it broke my heart.

I tried to tell Alex what Laura had just done, but Alex didn't want to hear it. In fact, he went as far as saying that maybe it was his fault since he'd been spending so much time with me.

"I think I have a future with Laura and I want her to be happy," Alex said. "I'm doing well in class now, and I think I will be okay from here on out. You've done a great job and have been a great friend, but I think it's time to wrap up our study sessions."

With tears rolling down my face, I could only stare dumbfounded, already realizing the depth of my loss. Alex gave me a side hug and a peck on the temple, then walked toward the door and into the arms of an impatient Laura while Michelle and Crystal stared me down.

After Alex and Laura walked into the gym, I called to Michelle and Crystal and screamed, "It's all over! I'm done tutoring Alex or trying to be his friend. I just want to be left alone! Do you hear me? It's over!"

Michelle barked back, "You've got that right. We know you won't be tutoring Alex anymore or talking to, hugging, or snuggling up to our best friend's boyfriend ever again.

"But it is far from over," she added. "It will never be over. Night-night, Droopy."

I knew she was telling the truth and that it would never end. Oh, wow, I'm really getting dizzy and am so sleepy. I wish my mom were here. I sure do need her now. Why do they hate me so much? Why is life so tough?

It's 10:00 a.m. This is my final journal entry.

∽

CHAPTER THREE

*K*athy let Chris sleep a little later that morning because she figured she was tired from the game and dance. Noon seemed late enough though. Surely she would be up for one of those juicy cheeseburgers from their favorite lunch spot down the street, Kathy thought.

After knocking on Chris' door a few times and not hearing a sound, Kathy entered the room with a "Wake up, Sleepyhead" followed by a scream that shook the entire neighborhood. Kathy looked on in unbelief and horror at her niece lying in a puddle of alcohol and covered in pills. Kathy immediately checked for a pulse and dialed 911.

Operator: "9-1-1. What's your emergency?"

Kathy: "My niece, my niece! She's unconscious! I don't think she's breathing!"

Operator: "Ma'am, can you tell me what is happening?"

Kathy: "My niece is lying on the floor of her bedroom. It looks like she took a bunch of pills."

Operator: "Ma'am, I am tracking your phone. Can you verify your address for me?"

Kathy: "It's 4447 Ridgemont Way, apartment number 113."

Operator: "Okay. Help is on the way. Are you there alone or is someone else with you?"

Kathy: "I am alone. It is just me and my niece."

Operator: "Can you tell me your name?"

Kathy: "Kathy, my name is Kathy."

Operator: "Okay, Kathy. We need to be certain whether or not she is breathing."

Kathy: "I can't tell. She's lying on her stomach."

Operator: "Kathy, I want you to gently roll her over to her back while protecting her head and neck."

Kathy: "Done."

Operator: "I need you to tilt her head back gently and look and listen for breathing. I also want you to check her chest to see if there is any movement."

Kathy: "She is not breathing."

Operator: "Does she have a pulse?"

Kathy: "No pulse either."

Operator: "Okay, Kathy. I want you to put your phone on speaker so I can talk with you while you begin CPR. Are you familiar with CPR?"

Kathy: "Yes, I am certified."

Operator: "Okay. I need you to apply chest compressions at a pace of about one compression every two seconds. Thirty compressions followed by two breaths. I need you to keep a steady pace. Can you do that for me?"

Kathy: "Yes, I can do that."

Operator: "I want you to continue CPR until help arrives. The paramedics are three minutes out."

Kathy: "Please hurry."

Operator: "You're doing great. Continue what you're doing but listen to me. When the paramedics arrive they will enter your house. I need you to call to them so they can find you quickly. I want you to continue CPR until they take over for you."

Kathy: "The door is unlocked. They should be able to make their way in."

It wasn't two minutes later that Kathy was calling out to the paramedics. "We are back here! We are here! We are here!"

When the paramedics arrived, they took over immediately. They called in all the information on Chris. Age, weight, sex … everything was moving so fast. They were loading her up and working on her and calling in the information all at the same time. Kathy had never seen anything like it before in her life.

"If you want to ride in the ambulance, you need to come with us now," one of the paramedics said to Kathy.

Kathy had barely hopped in the ambulance alongside Chris when the vehicle raced out of the complex with lights blazing and the siren blaring, speeding toward Marks General as fast as it possibly could.

"Please don't let her die, God," Kathy babbled over and over. "Please don't let her die."

CHAPTER FOUR

A Monday morning at Heights Central had not been that full of energy since the 2005 championship win late last year. The students were still pumped about Friday night's game and how the football team destroyed East Central forty-one to three before the big homecoming dance. The excitement continued as the tardy bell rang and the teachers started clearing the hallways. "Get to homeroom now" seemed to ring out in unison by teachers up and down the hall.

The familiar daily routine began. The teachers took attendance and marked tardies while the students chattered among themselves. This morning the assistant principal's morning announcements interrupted the homecoming reminiscing but, of course, that wasn't anything new. The announcements — or as Trevor liked to call them, "the crap they tell us that we don't really need to know but have to listen to anyway" — always marked the end of the fun conversations and the beginning of the boring stuff.

Trevor did manage to rile up his classmates one more time when it was time to hear the lunch choices of the day.

"Here comes the good part!" Trevor yelled.

The room erupted with a loud cheer upon hearing tater tots were the day's side to either pizza or meatloaf. The cheerleaders in the class got everyone fired up when they started cheering, "Tater tots, tater tots!"

Of course, it only lasted about ten seconds before Ms. Higgins shut down the celebration. Same thing every morning. Alex laughed and thought, *we really can be annoying sometimes,* as he gave Trevor a high five.

Before Alex and Trevor made it back to their seats, Principal Saunders' voice boomed through the PA system and everyone froze. Automatic silence filled the room. They knew something was wrong because they never heard him on the system unless there was a serious issue. Special assembly, auditorium, eight thirty. No one knew what it could be, but the general consensus was that it must be related to homecoming.

Alex looked at Trevor. "Anything you want to tell me?" Alex asked.

"It's not me this time," Trevor said with a bit of bite. But he had it coming because he was usually front and center with the annual homecoming pranks, and in most cases the mischief left the school officials up in arms.

Coach Carter nearly blew a gasket last year when he arrived at school the Monday after homecoming only to find that someone had planted a somewhat large oak tree in the middle of the football field. Coach never nailed the culprit, but it would be legendary to students for generations to come, just like Trevor dreamed. Another funny one was the time Principal Saunders' desk was moved to the teacher parking lot. That did not go over so well either.

Alex and Trevor punched and pushed each other as they made their way to the auditorium while reliving all the practical jokes they had coordinated. Well, that Trevor coordinated and Alex participated in. The timing of this particular assembly might prove to be one of the most difficult to get under control. As the seats began filling up, the noise level jolted and before long it seemed like the assembly might turn into a homecoming afterparty.

"Attention! May I have your attention? Please sit down and be quiet!" Principal Saunders screamed into the mic several times before he could use his inside voice again.

Students were required to sit with their homeroom classes and teachers, so Alex could not sit with Laura, but he did find her in the crowd, stood up with a goofy wave and blew her a big kiss from across the room.

"Sit down, Alex!" came the retort from the podium as the students roared in laughter. And it was back to the outside voice, "Quiet!!!!"

Ten minutes later than he anticipated starting the assembly, Principal Saunders needed to get the group under control. The counselors would be arriving at nine, and he knew it would take him several minutes to share with the students. He wanted to explain everything before they saw the group walk in — the adults who only show up when something tragic has happened.

"Please, I beg you. Please be respectful and listen," Principal Saunders whispered, glancing at his watch. Yelling wasn't working and he was emotionally spent anyway. With only fifteen minutes to spare, why not hope for a shred of human decency? And he was right. The soft-spoken request worked. The students settled down and listened quietly.

"There has been a tragedy in our school family," he began. "One of your classmates overdosed on pills over the weekend."

Gasps, unbelief, heads turning, eyes darting — and lots of confusion. "Who?" "Who was it?" "Who's not here today?" "Did you know anything about this?"

Hushing the students in a kinder, gentler tone this time, Principal Saunders launched into a grandfatherly discourse.

"I need you to take a moment and think about what I am telling you," he said. "Someone you know and come into contact with every day took enough pills to end her life because she was struggling and felt like she had no other way out.

"I don't know the whole story but I know that a tragedy like this should never happen," he continued. "Now, if I had to guess, there are many emotions running through this room right now. Some of you are scared right now, some of you are sad, and some of you will be angry. I see many of you looking around and wondering who is missing. We are providing counselors for anyone who would like to talk. We are encouraging anyone who might have been close to the victim to come forward if they have any information that can help us figure out exactly why this happened.

"I also want everyone in this room to know that regardless of what is going on in your life, you are special," Principal Saunders said, choking back tears. "Taking your life is not an option. It is not the answer. Please reach out and let us help you. My heart is broken, and this is something we will now have to deal with together as a school family."

Clenched fists, tear-welled eyes, and obvious anxiousness could be seen across the sea of high schoolers. They truly were trying to be respectful and hear all their principal had to say, but not knowing who it was was too much.

"Who overdosed?" one student finally yelled out in anger. His tone seemed insensitive but relief flooded the crowd because they all wanted to know.

"Christine," said Principal Saunders. "It was our new student Christine Ponders."

The buzz of conversation overtook the room as Mr. Saunders stepped aside to let the school's guidance counselor, Ms. Willis, take the platform.

"I have seen a lot of tragedy and dealt with many tough circumstances in my twenty-seven years as a guidance counselor," she began, "but I've never felt as sad as I do right now. It is a hard reality that one of the students at our school has taken her life. She is no longer alive. She has left people here who loved her, and I know her decision has left many of with questions. I want you to know that I am here to help you with anything you want or need to talk about. As Principal Saunders has already stated, taking your life should never be an option. I will be available for anyone who needs to talk."

As Principal Saunders came back to the podium to make some closing remarks, it was obvious that no one seemed to even know who Christine Ponders was — no one except Alex. It was taking everything he had not to throw up or pass out right there in his seat. "How could everyone be so confused?" he thought to himself. "Did no one else know Chris? Did she not have any friends? Had they not noticed her with me when we were studying?"

Laura was among those with a blank look on her face and asking those around her who Christine was. Michelle snarled her nose and Crystal rolled her eyes, both shrugging their shoulders and bored with the drama already, ready to get on to the next thing. But it was bugging Laura.

"Who is Christine?" she asked those in front of and behind her.

Finally a voice from two rows back said, "Droopy. You know, the girl you three loved to terrorize."

All three turned and stared at the kid they had never seen before — or at least never noticed — and tried to argue with him that it couldn't be. "Look around," he said. "Do you see her here?"

They desperately scanned the entire auditorium and then looked back at each other. They never heard another word from the podium or from the students around them as everyone cleared out to schedule a time with a counselor and then make their way back to class.

The big bad Triple Threat sat in silence, holding hands, paralyzed. Laura was barely able to take a breath. Not able to look at each other, the girls knew the truth in their hearts, and it was a feeling like nothing they had ever experienced before. The queens of icing out and isolating so many others in their path finally understood what true isolation felt like. It hurt, and they felt pure disgust at who they were and what they had done.

What have we done? Laura screamed in her head. *What have I done?*

CHAPTER FIVE

*A*lex shifted his attention to the cityscape view as the first burst of sunlight ushered in the new day. He had been up for a while relaxing in his favorite chair, sipping on his favorite French press coffee and quietly admiring the beauty of the luxury New York City loft surrounding him. Laura would not be up for a while so Alex planned to keep his regular Saturday morning ritual of preparing a hearty breakfast for one and settling in for a long day of football.

Taking a few more slow sips and letting his mind wander a bit, Alex thought about how much he loved the city. He loved everything from the Knicks to the traffic, the tall buildings to the noise. *The years have gone by too fast*, he thought, realizing he truly understood the old saying "in the blink of an eye."

Alex wondered if they could really be only three years away from thirty. *We are actual grown-ups*, he thought and laughed out loud, remembering some of the ridiculous stunts he and Trevor used to pull in high school.

Still, Alex knew he and Laura had truly accomplished good things since graduating from Heights Central almost ten years ago. They both attended Syracuse University and received a top-notch education. Alex was also able to fulfill his lifelong dream of playing football for the Orange. He paused his walk down memory lane for a moment to double-check the game time. Alex had not missed a Syracuse game since he was a teenager, and his spectator role rivaled the intensity he showcased as quarterback during his college days.

The pre- pre-game shows would be starting soon, so he decided he'd better get his breakfast prepared. He shook himself back to the current day and quietly slipped into the kitchen. The counter was a mess with the monthly gift basket of goodies left at the door by the homeowners association and several days' worth of mail piled up next to the basket. As Alex scooped up the envelopes and newspapers, he noticed a headline on Friday's paper about a local homecoming event. Mentions of high school homecoming games, parades, dances — anything homecoming really — always opened the old wound.

Would the Heights Central class of 2007 always have such a darkness draped over it? Would it ever get better? Judging by the atmosphere at the ten-year reunion during this year's homecoming football game a few weeks back, it didn't seem so.

"One tragic moment while we were teenagers took away all the good times, all the fun," he mumbled to himself with a bit of bitterness and an almost pouting tone. Laura was never the same after Chris committed suicide. While Alex had stuck by Laura through all the guilt and depression as they wrapped up high school, he often wondered how much better their lives would be if he had never befriended Chris.

If he and Chris had not been friends, then Laura would not have gotten jealous and likely would not have picked on her, Alex reasoned. Would that also mean Chris would be alive today? Alex couldn't decide but he felt sure that either way, he and Laura wouldn't be paying the price for the horrible decision Chris made.

Alex went through his own season of guilt, blaming himself for Chris' suicide because he pushed her away at the dance. His thoughts about the last things he said to her haunted him for weeks after that Monday morning announcement. *Why did I tell her I didn't need her anymore at the exact moment she was upset and needed me to encourage her? How could I have been so selfish, so focused on celebrating the win, that I didn't care about her pain?*

He managed to sleepwalk through the rest of his senior football season, but the team didn't make it to state. The players weren't really upset about it, however. None of the seniors seemed to care about much of anything.

With mid-term exams pressing in hard all around him in early December and still no relief from the guilt, Alex hit his lowest point and started researching how many pills it would take for someone of his size.

His mind wandered during the first half of the Christmas cantata — a tradition with his family and one his mom demanded not be broken no matter how many excuses he found that year. Alex cracked a smile during the opening number with the little kids because several of them were technically too young to participate and ended up going rogue, always difficult for the director but fun for the audience.

When, where and how to pull off his plan to relieve the pain forever hijacked his attention during the next few musical numbers, at least until intermission. He managed to paste on a fake smile and engage in chit chat with Deacon Gray and Mrs. Gray, the kindest person he had ever met. Mrs. Gray taught Alex in Sunday School when he was a child and is the one who helped him memorize the fruit of the Spirit.

Love, joy, peace, patience, self-control, kindness, gentleness ... no, no wait, love, joy, peace, patience, kindness, goodness, faithfulness, gentleness and self-control. That's the order, Alex chanted in his mind after Mrs. Gray turned to hug another former student. *Oh yeah, I've still got it,* Alex thought with a bit of swagger, losing himself to another time for a moment. The feedback squeal of the mic being readjusted on the stage brought him back to reality, now with even more ammunition to beat himself up. Not only had he been inconsiderate to Chris that night, he had gone against what God clearly outlined as the behaviors of one living for Jesus.

It was as if all he had learned in church and especially what he knew to be true since committing his life to Christ as a young 12 year old vanished with the excitement of winning that *stupid* homecoming game, he almost mumbled out loud, digging his fist into his leg hoping it would leave a deep and ugly bruise.

Flickering lights meant Alex had to hustle to splash some water on his face, breathe in some fresh air and climb over the family of six to settle back into his seat next to his dad. He slid in just as the pastor handed the still squealing mic to the orchestra director to introduce the opening number of the second half of the cantata.

Assuming he would escape back to his mind games, Alex swallowed hard when the tone of the stringed instruments pierced his soul as the musicians seamlessly flowed from one number to the next. He couldn't take his eyes off the violinist and then the flute and then the simplicity of the piano keys filling the entire auditorium alone.

"Stand and sing the final number with us," the music director announced, startling Alex who had been lulled into an almost hypnotic state. The little girl sitting next to Alex snickered when he jumped. Embarrassed and feeling the heat rise in his face, he winked at her and shuffled his shoulders a few more times to cover. Of course, that only caused more disruption because she laughed out loud and then everyone on his pew as well as the pew in front of him turned to look.

Alex's mom caught his eye but instead of the glaring "you had better straighten up" look, she smiled really big and nodded. It was as if she knew she had her Alex back. Something changed in Alex's heart in that half hour of Christmas music. The draw was familiar and the release of the guilt made him whole again. He whispered a thank you to Christ for His grace, removing the pain and making a way for us to forgive ourselves. *Happy Birthday, my Lord.*

Joining in a little late on that last song, Alex stood and belted out loudly:

> Be near me, Lord Jesus, I ask Thee to stay
> Close by me forever, and love me, I pray
> Bless all the dear children in Thy tender care,
> And take us to Heaven, to live with Thee there.

Back in the New York City loft, Alex remained confident in his own healing from the guilt of Chris' suicide, but he still wondered about how things might have been different if he had not made that one decision to ask Chris to tutor him. He also desperately wanted Laura to find peace.

"Will Laura ever heal?" Alex asked no one in particular but then turned it into a prayer. "God, you know I've begged you for Laura to get over this every day since it happened. I really don't know how to help her. Please help her."

The idea of moving away popped back into his head. It had been an idea he and Laura had toyed with for a few years. Her counselor suggested it might be helpful. This was one of the rare snippets of information Laura shared with Alex from one of the hundreds of counseling sessions she had had since that first sit-down with a grief counselor that fateful day in high school.

I don't know if it will really help, but I'm desperate, Alex thought. *I am willing to give anything a try.*

Moving far away was the strategy for the other two-thirds of Triple Threat.

Crystal left as soon as she could after high school graduation. She never attended college but landed in Los Angeles working as a waitress and trying to pick up any acting gigs she could find.

Michelle was in Texas. She and Trevor both attended the University of Texas and got married after college. They loved Austin and seemed to be doing well.

It wasn't until the ten-year reunion that Alex realized the torturous guilt all three still carried. Even though Alex and Laura had managed to see Trevor and Michelle at least twice a year since high school, at the time of the reunion, Laura, Michelle, and Crystal had not all three been together in years. They had wanted their own mini-reunion ahead of the full class reunion. They met for lunch the day of the big event, spent the afternoon shopping for the perfect outfits, and helped each other get ready (like old times) so they could be strong for each other when it was time to make their appearance. They were the famous Triple Threat, after all.

CHAPTER SIX

*F*or a few hours before the reunion, Triple Threat snapped back into their pre-Chris personas and were only worried about being the most beautiful and envied alumnae at the reunion. They even giggled and danced around some as they put the finishing touches on their hair. But the momentary reprieve from pain only lasted until about three seconds after they pranced through the gymnasium doors.

Instead of the stunned silence of a roomful of past peers staring in awe, they walked into a wall of disgust and distaste.

Michelle scurried over to Trevor to take refuge from the endless sea of piercing eyes. Crystal slipped over to a side group of random alums' kids playing in the floor and chatted away mindlessly, hoping everyone would forget she was there. But Laura, oh Laura! She just stood there in the main entranceway, paralyzed, all alone and mentally back in the auditorium realizing what had just happened and knowing she was the cause.

After what seemed like hours, Alex snapped out of his own stupor and calmly walked over to Laura, put his arm around her, and guided her over to the punch bowl, but she refused to take a sip. She didn't want to sit down; she didn't want to talk to anyone. She just wanted to stand there and stare. Her eyes — absolutely empty and filled with deep pain — finally darted across the room, soaking up all the faces and targeting her escape. Before Alex could put his punch cup down, Laura bolted for the door and didn't stop running for seven blocks. Alex almost didn't catch her. When he did, she swore that was the last time she would ever set foot on the campus of Heights Central.

But a week later Alex decided to test how serious Laura really was because he seriously needed to go back one more time.

Coach Carter just announced his retirement and there was going to be a party and celebration in his honor. Every student who had ever played for him would be invited, so it would definitely be a great sendoff for him.

Alex couldn't believe Coach Carter was actually retiring. He was one of those timeless legends for those who played for him, and Alex just had to be part of the retirement celebration. Trevor felt the same way, so they worked tirelessly all week to convince Laura and Michelle.

"We need to be there for Coach. He has done so much for us," Alex had said to Laura. "Remember how he stayed up on my college career and sent me notes of encouragement every week? Plus, our class was extra special to him in general. I'm not sure why he liked us so much, but he did."

"We just can't miss this reunion," he had said, almost in tears and on the verge of anger that he was having to work so hard to get her to understand how important this was to him. After all, he had sacrificed so much over the years just because Laura didn't feel like doing this or wasn't interested in doing that.

Moments before Alex lashed out at Laura this past Thursday, a sliver of compassion emerged and she gave in — with stipulations.

Michelle and Crystal both had to attend. If he could make that happen, then the reunion was a go.

Alex had scurried to call Trevor to discover that Michelle had softened as well and agreed. Michelle yelled in the background that she had just heard from Crystal, who said she would go with them. Alex had hung up the phone with a smile on his face.

That smile continued until the the last set of commercials before today's kickoff. He sat reflecting and thought how this time next week they would be getting ready for the big event.

About that time, Alex heard the floorboards squeaking, and he was excited that his Laura was up and moving. Maybe they could just snuggle up and watch some football. It was going to be a great day, a great week. *I can't wait to see the old gang,* Alex thought.

Alex's mood took an immediate shift when he saw the look of horror on Laura's face as she turned the corner into the living room.

"What is it?" Alex asked.

Laura handed him her phone and fell on the couch, curling up into a ball with tears running down her cheeks. Alex was in disbelief as he read the text message from Michelle. Crystal had been in a car accident. They were saying it was drug- and alcohol-related. She was killed instantly.

Alex couldn't get Laura to eat or even get out of bed for the next week except to attend Crystal's funeral on Wednesday. On the way home, he gathered the courage to ask Laura if she was still open to attending the reunion. But within seconds, he wished he had not asked.

She swore that if he ever mentioned the reunion or Heights Central ever again it would be the last thing he ever did. Alex believed her and knew in his heart they would never visit the old high school again.

Alex plummeted into a bit of depression of his own for a few days but then pulled himself out of it and decided he would channel his energy into caring for his wife rather than trying to relive the good ol' days. He became obsessed with wiping out the guilt that tortured Laura. He was determined to remove all that was haunting her, and it would start with a change of scenery.

"A fresh start is what we need," Alex concluded. "And I'm going to make that happen."

CHAPTER SEVEN

*S*alt Lake City was more beautiful than he imagined. It was no New York City and part of Alex would always remain there. His mind jumped to how neighbors rallied around one another after the tragedy of 9/11 and all the time that was spent in prayer and seeking God during that time. Yeah, Alex had a real connection to New York and the people, but he could tell he was really learning to love Utah as well. The air was so clean you could almost feel it purifying your lungs. At least it felt that way to Alex.

It was a Saturday morning and Alex was still an early riser. He took inventory of all the projects he needed to be working on around the house. They had been here almost eight months now and it was more than time to start settling in, especially since their firstborn would be arriving any day.

It was so different living in a huge home and keeping up with everything that came with it. In the loft, Alex never had to worry about cutting the grass, taking care of the pool, keeping the garage clean, or trimming the bushes, but Laura fell in love with the house the minute she saw it. The whole point of the move was to help her heal and improve her spirit and mood, so Alex was going to do whatever it took. Laura continued to struggle with depression, and pregnancy hormones had only made it worse, but Alex felt confident that bringing a new baby home to a house she loved would change everything for Laura. He just had to survive a few more days.

Survival sometimes meant not living in the reality of the moment. Alex loved to let his mind drift back to his glory days at Syracuse. He had lots of friends and absolutely loved playing college football. Alex received an athletic scholarship while Laura had managed a partial academic scholarship, but money was not an issue. Their scholarships were more a matter of accomplishment than need.

Alex's family always encouraged him to make his own way, and Laura's mother believed it is important for women to be able to support themselves financially regardless of family wealth or how much money their husbands make. She always pushed Laura to find her own way and reach for success, but when Laura followed in her footsteps of studying interior design, she couldn't have been prouder. Alex and Laura were a masterful team with all the right connections, so the move across the country did mean Laura would have to start over to some degree. Alex left his own lucrative position as well, but he walked right into another high-end job with a highly accredited architectural firm, so his transition wasn't going to be quite as unnerving. Alex believed the job with Landing Architects was a perfect fit and was thrilled they felt the same way about him.

Still, they would have never left their life on the East Coast if it had not been for that tragedy so long ago. *Has it really been more than twelve years already?* Alex wondered.

Alex turned thirty last month while Laura was still a youngster at twenty-nine-and-a-half — at least that's the way she referred to herself in comparison to Alex — and that awful experience had been part of their lives every day since their late teens. No matter what he was thinking about, Alex's mind always went back to that tragic day. For the first few years, it angered him that he couldn't get Laura to grasp the concept of forgiveness and letting go of the guilt, but he eventually conceded that it would always be attached to her, and thus, to him. He hadn't decided which was worse — watching Laura be haunted by it daily or how her pain affected him.

In fact, it was the years of counseling and more prescription medication than he could count that convinced Alex they needed to get as far away from that memory as they possibly could. And there they were, about as far away as they could get without crossing an ocean. They were 2,200 miles west of New York City via I–80, a thirty-three-hour drive to be exact, and had officially traded in tall buildings, crowded streets, and the hustle of big city life for majestic mountains, open roads, and a whole lot of calm.

Alex snapped out of his daydreaming and decided it was time to get busy and do some much-needed work in the yard. As he headed for the hedge trimmers, he saw the stack of unpacked boxes that still needed attention. He also questioned why he was doing all the work himself. Yes, the exercise wouldn't hurt him at all, but why not follow in Laura's parents' footsteps and hire people to do all the household chores? *After all, they even hired people to change the channels on their TV,* he smirked. Why should he not be willing to finance people who needed work as well, he was thinking as he chuckled to himself.

Alex and Laura were set financially, so hiring people to help around the house would be easy. Along with each of their incomes and the inheritance they would receive from Laura's family one day, they now had Alex's trust fund, which became his on that recent 30th birthday. The stipulation for receiving full access to the trust fund was that he had graduated from college, found a steady job, and stayed with that job for at least five years. Those conditions were easy for Alex. He loved school, he loved playing football, and his love for architecture made his work feel like a fun hobby rather than work.

So, hiring help around the house was something Alex considered often, but the truth was that he wasn't in a hurry to get everything organized. The unpacked boxes, unending yard work, and other random projects were a good distraction, maybe even an escape, from Laura. Alex confessed to himself that the list of things to do was a productive way to spend less time with her without looking like he was trying to avoid her. *Just a few more days*, he chanted, *just a few more days*. "We've made the move across the country. She loves our new home, and once the baby arrives, we can start over with an entirely new life," he told himself. Holding out hope for this "entirely new life" was the only thing keeping him from going insane.

Laura had spent almost every hour outside of work wrapped up in the covers in the dark, and usually with the home shopping network running on the TV.

At least the past few weeks have somewhat justified her being in bed since she is nine months pregnant and as big as this 6,200-square-foot mansion we call a home, thought Alex.

Before she got pregnant, Laura would make time for exercise with a small circle of friends at the YMCA, but she pulled away from that soon into the pregnancy. Now the only exercise she got was to get dressed for work — when she decided to take on a new client, which was not too often at the time.

They were caught in a constant stream of lies about why Laura rarely left the house. She tried to avoid people at all costs. She even pushed her parents away before the move, but they knew the source of her grief and so they always gave her a pass.

How much I miss the girl I knew who was so full of life in high school, Alex thought with a deep sadness attached. *Isn't there something in the Bible I could get her to read about accepting God's forgiveness?*

Alex honestly couldn't remember much of what he used to know about God's word, and he felt a twinge of guilt for not staying better connected to God and failing to keep God's word in front of Laura. But she hasn't been interested and he doesn't really know what to say. He managed to still pray for her in the worst moments. He really did love her deeply, even when she was ugly to him. He also loved how beautiful she was and the feeling of every guy's jealously that she was his.

Being good looking sure can make up for a lot, Alex thought with a small laugh. *I just really thought we could truly be happy. Maybe with us finally settling into this move and the baby on the way, Laura can start to come out of her depression.*

He was just about to trim the hedges when he heard the scream from the upstairs window. It was time. The baby was on the way.

CHAPTER EIGHT

*A*lex tripped up the stairs, and Laura was already criticizing him while screaming in agony. "What took you so long?"

"I came as quickly as I could!" Alex exclaimed.

"Get dressed now!" Laura shouted back. "Why can't you be ready when I need you? I need you to focus on me right now and stop thinking about yourself."

Alex bit his tongue, but what he wanted to say was, "All I ever do is focus on you. It's all about you and has been for a very long time. What happened to the person I wanted to marry so long ago? Where is the Laura who thought I hung the moon and wanted to marry me more than anything else in this world? That girl would have never treated me this way."

Instead, he responded, "You're right. I should have been ready. I'm all yours. Let's get to the car."

By now Laura was upset and a mess with her water breaking. There was no use in using kind sentiments like, "You look beautiful" or "You're doing great." Alex knew they would be wasted on her anyway. He wondered why he should even try.

"Did you get the right suitcase?" she asked, which snapped him out of his discussion with himself. "My medication. Did you bring my medication?"

Alex assured her it was all covered.

"That would be a first," Laura snapped.

As Alex helped Laura through the door to the garage and down the steps, he nearly broke into a panic when he realized he grabbed the key to the Corvette and not the minivan. He took Laura to the van, which fortunately was unlocked so he was able to get Laura seated.

"I grabbed the wrong key," he said. "I'll be right back. I'll hurry."

"Idiot!" she shouted. "I need you to get it together."

Alex frantically rushed back into the house and looked through the number of keys hanging on the wall. BMW, no. Lexus, no. F-150, no. Minivan keys, yes. Alex quickly grabbed the keys and clipped them to his home and office key ring, the one he always has on him, then hurried back, loaded the suitcase in the car, opened the garage door, cranked the car, and screeched out of the garage.

"Here we go, Baby!" Alex shouted. "Just concentrate on your breathing. We will be there soon."

Back inside his head, Alex continued his conversation with himself. *We are finally off to the hospital for this beautiful moment in our lives. I wish my wife would cut me some slack. At least traffic isn't too crazy because — heaven forbid — that would be one more thing that is my fault.*

Dr. Dekal finally answered the OnStar call and snapped Alex out of his pity party. "How far apart are the contractions?" Dr. Dekal asked Alex.

"I have no idea," Alex shouted to the dashboard. "They are close!"

"Okay, stay calm and get to the hospital safely. We still have plenty of time. I just need you not to panic," Dr. Dekal responded. "I'll meet you there. You remember where to pull up for labor and delivery, right?"

"Of course, I know," Alex said in disgust as he hung up on Laura's doctor.

Laura snarled and was about to say something sarcastic when Alex's key ring caught her eye. "Luke 8:17, what does that mean again?" Laura asked Alex instead of biting his head off. "I remember when your mom gave that to you. I didn't realize you still had it."

Before Alex could answer, another contraction hit and Laura was screaming in pain. "Hold on, Baby. Hold on. We are almost there."

Within minutes he swung into the labor and delivery entrance relieved to be greeted by two really sweet — and calm — nurses. It was a team effort getting Laura settled, but something miraculous happened as Alex handed Laura off to the nurses. She looked up at Alex with those beautiful eyes he loved so much and a calm demeanor he had not experienced in years. "Alex," she said as tears streamed down her face. "I love you so much and could not be more thankful to have you as my husband. Thank you for loving me."

Paralyzed and absolutely stunned, Alex stuttered as the nurses looked on with tears of their own. "I know," he finally spit out. "Everyone should be as lucky as us. We are truly blessed." He wasn't sure if he really believed that but knew he certainly wanted to believe it.

Laura blew Alex a kiss as she was wheeled through the sliding doors out of Alex's sight. He returned the gesture and scurried back to the driver's seat to park the minivan and hurry in to meet back up with Laura.

"It's going to be okay," Alex told himself with a fist pump and an extra oomph as he repeated it out loud. "It is going to be okay!"

CHAPTER NINE

*A*lex was sitting quietly in the chair next to Laura and Ben as they both slept. It was August 23, and Baby Ben had finally arrived. Twenty-six hours of intensive labor for Laura. *And for me,* Alex thought sarcastically.

Staring over at their new beautiful eight pound, seven ounce baby boy, Alex had finally slowed down enough to realize that he was now a father. He couldn't take his eyes off Baby Ben even though he was physically exhausted. Alex's body desperately wanted rest, but his mind would not settle down. His thoughts were all over the place, like how he and Laura never liked hospitals and yet here they both were. His mind then went to how uncomfortable the reclining side chair was but how he didn't think he could sleep right now even if he were in a Ritz-Carlton king-size bed.

"I need sleep," Alex said to himself one minute, and then the next minute he would turn around and argue with himself that he didn't. *You will be home in less than 24 hours and you can sleep then. Or wait! Will we ever sleep again? Oh no! How are we going to rest now that we have a baby? Will we take turns sleeping? I'm not sure I can function on no sleep. I'm so tired. I'm not tired. I can do this. You can do this, Alex. Man up.*

Alex's mind continued scurrying around in a hundred different directions with each new thought stomping on the previous ones. He finally settled down into a light slumber as he thought of the fresh start their newly expanded family would have now. He drifted a little deeper with sweet dreams of Baby Ben.

"No, not sweet and simple," Alex almost yelled out loud before sucking back the words about to come out of his mouth. The thought jolted him awake about the same time his head fell from its perch and startled him.

Life was already complicated for us and we just added a new dimension to it, Alex thought. *Laura can barely take care of herself. How is she going to handle being a mother?*

Of course, Alex knew he also wasn't really ready for this new season in life. "We do love you, little guy," Alex whispered toward Ben. "We just weren't quite ready for you."

Snapping out of his somberness, Alex starting chuckling to himself, thinking about the fact that they were surprised to get pregnant. Lack of protection, spontaneity, and a strong sex drive might not have been the best combination if they weren't ready to get pregnant, he surmised.

It's almost confusing just how much Alex and Laura enjoyed their sex life when everything else about their marriage had been so difficult. In some ways, making love may have been an escape for Laura. It and sleep were the only times she could truly not be consumed by the tragedy that would forever haunt her.

Alex was thankful to have a wife who enjoyed sex. He often thought of the words of his best friend and partner in crime, Trevor Williams. "If your sex life is good, everything else will take care of itself." At least that was Trevor's philosophy.

Alex could still see Trevor's mischievous wink after saying things like that, the wink that usually meant they were both about to get in trouble. Oh, the trouble those two could find, and always at Trevor's leading. Alex wondered how he was so easily influenced by Trevor, someone who didn't have a serious bone in his body. He just knew that he really loved that guy and always had fun when they were together.

Alex's mind jumped to the struggles Trevor and Michelle had in their marriage. Trevor had confided in Alex along the way, and when Alex opened up about his concerns, Trevor always blew it off. When Alex recently shared his anxiety and fear of becoming a father, Trevor acted concerned at first and then came out with the most unsympathetic response: "Oh boo hoo, you big rich man with your great job and beautiful wife. You're breaking my heart."

The concerns were real for Alex, but he really didn't have anyone he could truly talk to about them, and it was his own fault. The Alex and Laura everyone in the outside world knew were quite different from what their lives were really like. Only those closest to them would ever know of the struggles they were having, and even then Alex and Laura were able to put on a good show most of the time.

Yes, we are the couple that has it all, Alex often thought to himself. *Just like Oprah and Dr. Phil holding the key to life.*

The real Alex and Laura were actually quite a mess, so much so that they could be main characters in a book or movie, he thought. It's not from a lack of love for each other, Alex confirmed in his own mind. His anxiety and frustrations and Laura's depression all stemmed from her inability to accept God's forgiveness as well as forgive herself and start living again.

Alex loved to think back to the first time he saw Laura. There they were at Mountain Zion Baptist Church. Her family had just moved into the city and visited one Sunday. His family clicked with her family almost immediately. Lucky for Alex, they loved Pastor Mark and never wanted to attend anywhere else. They had no idea that same church would be the location of their wedding one day. It was a place they both loved. They had so many fond memories of great events and great times taking place in that building throughout their youth and adult lives.

The Maddox family and the Stewarts did just about everything together, and Alex and Laura were inseparable. They were in middle school at the time and neither one of them was really interested in dating, but they were not interested in spending any time apart either.

Alex was really involved in football and basketball, but he really excelled at football. Laura was dancing and cheering, and by the time they had reached their senior year of high school, they were most definitely interested in dating and right where a power couple should be — at the top of the food chain.

They came from wealthy families, had nice cars and fancy clothes, and were straight A students. To top it all off, Laura was head cheerleader and Alex was captain of the football team. The local papers reported almost weekly about Alex Maddox, the kid with the golden arm.

No power couple would be complete without being named king and queen of the homecoming court. Alex's and Laura's parents tried to keep them grounded and made sure they were in church every Sunday. Both sets of parents were adamant about Alex and Laura remaining humble and being thankful for all they had. And the big one was no sex before marriage. To the shock of most of their friends, they honored that commitment through high school, college, and their engagement.

Alex would often think about how he and his new wife of just a few hours had no clue what they were doing at nine thirty-seven p.m. on July 9th, 2012, in that beautiful cabin in the mountains, but it sure was fun figuring it out.

The memory took Alex far away from the current reality, deep into the sweet moments of his honeymoon with Laura. A whimper from Ben snapped Alex back to reality.

"It's okay, little guy," Alex whispered as he checked on the baby. "I'm going to protect you from the kind of pain and hurt that your mommy has endured. I just wish I could protect your mommy, too."

But Alex knew Laura was reaping the result of her own doing, and there was really nothing he could do. They could have had it all if not for the crazy jealousy Laura had toward Chris in high school. It was so unmerited, so unnecessary. There was just no reason for it, and now Alex and Laura had to relive that horrific tragedy over and over and over.

Why did Chris have to commit suicide? It would have gotten better, Alex replayed in his mind. *Even though I upset her at the homecoming dance, she knew I appreciated her and my conscience is clear. At least it should be, right? I think that's true. I hope it's true.*

But Laura. Why that lapse in judgment? Why so mean to Chris all the time? Why so ugly for no reason? Alex just couldn't understand it. Laura had been through it a hundred times with the counselor. She checked all the good girl boxes and was held in high esteem among the church youth group leaders. She wasn't perfect, however, and she chose not to discipline the ugly side of her that surfaced in high school. Still, everyone else has extended grace to her — she was young and she made a mistake. Why would that mistake not go away?

Why even now at this important time in their lives was that tragedy the very thing that would not leave them alone?

CHAPTER TEN

*T*he numbers on his phone said it was two minutes after three in the morning and Alex still could not close his eyes. He began thinking about how life never stops. There are no breaks. Good, bad, happy, and sad — life never slows down and we have no choice but to always do our best to keep up, Alex thought.

"Is it wrong for Laura and me to get to live a full life when Chris' life ended so suddenly?" he asked himself, feeling a bit emotional and melancholy now.

Crystal popped into his mind as well. She never had the chance to fulfill her dreams either. *What gave us the right to fulfill ours when so many others never get the chance?*

Rubbing his temples, Alex wondered why these questions stirred in his mind. So much fresh guilt, but why now? He had much bigger things to be worrying about, and he really needed some sleep. This had to be the tiredness coming through, he thought, but battling the guilt was his father's voice chatting the family motto: "We are the Maddoxes and the Maddoxes never give up."

It was true. The Maddox family always pushed through the tough days somehow.

I know in the world's eyes we have it all, Alex thought, *but the more success we achieve, the heavier Laura's guilt becomes. It seems to be the price we are paying, and now we have this little one to care for so we must find a way to continue to push forward.*

Alex's mind jumped back to their sophomore year in college when Laura's depression dipped really low. He'd worked so hard to keep her motivated. He could feel the anger and bitterness from those days rising back to the surface.

Alex felt like he'd had so much on him already that Laura should have been his support, not the other way around. "We should have been partners," he thought. "Not just one of us carrying all the weight all the time."

He remembered how Laura's counseling sessions increased from twice a month in high school to once a week in college and how she was put on medication but wasn't getting better. She had had twice-a-week appointments for the last three years, and yet she was still on a plateau.

Internally, his emotions shifted from anger to bitterness to sadness to hopefulness to determination — *If not for us, then we'll do it for Ben.*

But Alex knew the road ahead would not be easy. After all, if they were battling as many demons as they were with all the privileges and advantages they had had in life, how could they protect little Ben?

If only his love for Laura could be enough to keep her encouraged, steady, and strong, Alex pondered.

"I really think I've sacrificed and sacrificed beyond what anyone would ever expect, but she still wants her pills," he grumbled almost out loud. "She seems to trust them more than me and that makes me really …"

Before he finished his thought, his mind did a one-eighty and remembered that Laura had been off the medication throughout the pregnancy and would continue to go without the pills while breastfeeding. That should mean a full year without the medication that she had become so dependent on. Might this be the break they needed?

It was difficult for her to take the step to go off the medication, but she did it for Ben, so that must mean there was some strength buried down deep in her somewhere.

An obnoxious yawn distorted Alex's face as he looked over at Laura and Ben both sleeping soundly. Envious of how calm they both seemed, he knew he had to settle his mind and get some rest.

As he snuggled into a more comfortable position, he began to visualize a daily routine with a baby. *I'm not sure we can actually do this without someone to help us*, he realized.

Laura refused to be a stay-at-home mother and would be looking to return to work as soon as possible. She would also be obsessed with getting her body back in shape. She always said, "If I don't look good, then no one is going to hire me to make their home or office look good."

Thinking about work steered Alex's attention to his own assignments and spurred him to grab a nearby scratch pad and pen to jot down a to-do list. A possible new account was coming his way and he quickly outlined everything he could think of related to the upcoming schedule and what the account would mean.

The Landing had a meeting with the ownership and talent of KYCL Radio in three months. The station hosted one of the most famous talk shows, Darcy Dishes It Out, and was looking to build a new station downtown. It was one of those accounts every firm dreamed of.

Alex's boss said that if they were fortunate enough to land this account, Alex's team would be taking point. Even though the timing fell right after Ben's birth, the next few weeks would be crucial as the team prepared for the presentation. It would demand his full attention to land the biggest account of his career.

But first things first, Alex thought as he began to nod off. *I must find some help, and fast.*

He ticked off a list of things to do, starting with determining exactly which positions were needed to help them run their household. From there, he would need to advertise the position and begin interviewing the best candidates.

"For the nanny position, it needs to be a super nanny," Alex determined. "We need someone special to help raise our son, and most likely finish raising us in the process."

After glancing back over his list of things to do, he wanted to give in to panic, something unusual for him, but instead he decided to try something else out, something he hadn't done lately — pray.

CHAPTER ELEVEN

*I*t was August 24 around ten in the morning and the twenty-four-hour discharge period was rapidly approaching. Alex, Laura, and Baby Ben would soon be on their way home from the hospital. While it had been only forty-eight hours since leaving the house to welcome Baby Ben, the new parents felt like they had been there for weeks.

The rain was coming down in buckets, and the air outside was chilling to the bone. Regardless of the weather, Alex needed a moment to calm himself so he grabbed an umbrella from guest services and decided to take a little stroll outside the hospital to gather his thoughts before the ride home. Picking back up on the prayer he started last night as he drifted off to sleep, Alex thanked God for Ben and Laura and asked for help about the next steps.

He looked around at the scenery as he strolled in the rain thinking how calm it felt here and how different it was from New York. *Maybe I am getting used to this place*, Alex thought. *I hope Ben will love it here. Who knows? Maybe he will be a Utah Jazz fan.* About that time, Alex received a text from the nurses' station alerting him that it was time to check out, so he hurried back to sign the paperwork while Laura finished getting ready in the room.

The CNAs giggled nervously as they gathered up flowers and gifts for Laura. In spite of just going through an intensive labor process, Laura looked stunning. She intimidated everyone in her path. But even with all the confidence that showed on the outside, underneath was a woman terrified about being a new mother. She was almost paralyzed with fear when she thought about the fact that the decisions she made from now on were going to impact this child for the rest of his life.

What scared her even more was the thought of all the things she knew her child would face growing up. How could she be there to protect him from the world? The mere thought of it just made her want to vomit. She knew firsthand how cruel the world could be.

There was a time in her life when Laura would have turned to prayer and let God help her with her worries. She was a believer and they did attend church some, but Laura knew she had strayed far from her trust in God and wondered if He would even hear her prayers.

It was now ten fifteen and Alex had just finished up the paperwork at the nurses' station and was being greeted with many congratulations from all the staff and even a couple of strangers.

Sasha, the nurse who had been taking such good care of the Maddox family in spite of Laura's complaining, arrived at the nurses' station with a wheelchair and asked Alex if he was ready to go get his family. Alex gave a hesitant nod and they proceeded toward the room.

When they arrived at the room, Laura was sitting at the end of her hospital bed while Ben was sleeping peacefully in the crib next to her.

Sasha looked at Ben and said, "Hey, little man. You are so beautiful."

She then locked the wheels on the chair, looked at Laura and did a little curtsy. "Your chariot awaits, my lady," she said with a smile and a wink.

Laura rolled her eyes, scooted off the bed, told Alex to get her makeup bag, and sat down in the wheelchair.

Sasha stepped over to the bed where Ben was lying and picked him up ever so gently. She gave him a kiss on the forehead and said, "May God bless you, sweet little Ben. May He guide you and protect you all of your days." After a slight pause, she added, "You take care of your mommy and daddy. They are going to need your help."

Although Laura said nothing to Sasha, she found that moment to be very special. She was touched by the love and care this stranger was showing for her child. Laura could see she truly cared for Ben.

Sasha handed Ben to Laura and, wiping tears from her eyes, unlocked the wheels. Alex grabbed the makeup bag and the four of them proceeded toward the car. When they arrived at the walkway, Sasha waited with Laura and Ben while Alex went to get the car. He had loaded all of their other items earlier when he did the final preparations to the car for Ben's ride home.

When Alex pulled up under the overhang, he opened the passenger doors. Sasha inspected the car seat and gave some quick instructions while showing Alex how to buckle in baby Ben. She gave each of them a hug and gently closed the car doors so she would not disturb Ben's sleep.

As the new Maddox party of three drove away, the staff that was so helpful at Marks General Hospital was waving and blowing them kisses. As Alex headed toward the freeway, Laura stared in silence, trying to absorb all that had just happened and thinking about this new chapter in their lives.

CHAPTER TWELVE

*I*t had been about five minutes since Alex and Laura had left the hospital and neither of them had spoken a word.

Alex looked up and noticed a bigger-than-life billboard sign with none other than Darcy Campbell's picture.

"That is the station we are trying to get the new account with at work," Alex said.

"That would be good," Laura said in a less than enthusiastic voice. "I hope it works out for you."

"It will be good for our family," Alex said in a kind voice despite his frustration. "This is a huge account. Do you mind if we listen to the station for a few minutes?" Laura agreed, and Alex was thankful to have something to break up the silence.

"Just don't turn it up too loud," Laura said. "Ben is sleeping."

Alex made sure the volume was low before turning on the radio to KYCL, where the station was heading to commercial.

"This is KYCL and you are listening to Darcy Campbell. We will return with Darcy Dishes It Out after the break. Stay with us."

Alex told Laura he had been hearing about this show Darcy Dishes It Out, and he had been wanting to hear what all the fuss was about.

"I see her face plastered everywhere," Laura said. "I wouldn't mind checking her out." She looked at Alex and said with a sassy voice, "Let's just see what old Darcy is dishing out."

It was about ten thirty a.m. so KYCL would be re-airing the episode from the day's previous show. They ran Darcy live every day from four to six p.m. for drive-time traffic and then replayed the show the following morning from ten until noon.

After about two minutes of commercials, the intro music started to play and the most beautiful voice Alex had ever heard said, "Welcome back listeners. I am Darcy Campbell, and you are listening to Darcy Dishes It Out."

As she continued to talk, Alex was drawn to her voice. He had seen her pictures and how attractive she was but something about her voice was almost mesmerizing. Alex began to think about the account and how he could possibly even have the opportunity to work with this woman. He thought they may even have a chance to become friends.

Just then the car next to them honked as Alex started to veer out of his lane. Alex immediately snapped out of his fantasy world and brought himself back to reality as Laura gave him the evil eye.

"Sorry," said Alex, "just tired I guess." Focusing back on his driving, Alex continued to listen to Darcy as she told a little bit about the show.

Darcy explained, "For any of you who are new listeners out there, on this show we like to cover a wide range of topics. I would also like to clarify that we are not a show with cheap gossip. We want to discuss real topics with real substance that is relevant to our listeners.

"My job is to listen to people's points of view and then tell them when they are wrong." Darcy was now laughing as she said, "Isn't that right, Cheryl?"

Cheryl was Darcy's longtime producer who did a great job running the phone lines and making sure to get the best possible calls on the air.

"Speaking of wrong," Cheryl said, "Jim from Riverton is on line two and he is a little fired up about some of our topics from last week."

"Big surprise," said Darcy. Jim was a regular caller. Darcy couldn't stand him but he was good for ratings. "Hey Jim. You're live with Darcy. What you got for me today?"

"I'll tell you what I have, Darcy. What I have is a sick stomach after listening to some of the garbage you are supporting these days."

"Do tell," said Darcy.

"The big topic on last week was all this sexual harassment going on in the news," said Jim. "Now I know a lot of it is for real but the truth is a lot of these women are trying to get their piece of the pie."

"Let me stop you right there, Jim," Darcy interrupted.

"No, Darcy. I called in to talk, so I'm gonna talk and you gonna listen. Why now are all these women coming out? Twenty years is too long to keep a secret and then all of a sudden decide it's time to share. Money. It is all about money."

"Jim, you need to shut it now and listen," said Darcy. As Jim tried to continue, Darcy's voice got perpetually louder. "Shut up, Jim, and listen," Darcy said. "I have never been through anything like what these women have experienced."

"They're making it up," Jim said emphatically.

"I said shut up, Jim, and listen," Darcy barked back. "I have never been through anything like what these women have experienced, but as a woman I can tell you I would be humiliated to be treated that way. In so many of these cases these women are being abused by men they trust, men who are supposed to be protective of them and looking out for their well-being. The courage these women are showing is heroic and I'll tell you why."

"Do tell," Jim said in a tone that had the audience seeing him roll his eyes through the radio.

"Because every time one of these women speaks up, it helps to prevent the possibility of it happening to someone else," Darcy continued. "No human being has the right to ruin another human being's dreams or take away their feelings of self-worth."

"Darcy, I just think you're bitter because no one has hit on you in a while," Jim said.

"I won't justify that with a comment. I'm disconnecting you now, Jim. When you have something productive to say, call back and we can discuss it."

"How about we discuss it over dinner? It would be my pleasure to sexually harass you." As Jim was laughing, the phone line was disconnected.

Cheryl chimed in, "Well, that was pleasant," she said sarcastically.

"Be his pleasure to sexually harass me? Ugh. I think I just threw up in my mouth," Darcy said. "And I'll tell you something else, Jim. It would be my pleasure to kick your sorry redneck … "

"Try Wendy's new bacon double cheeseburger," blared out as Cheryl switched over to a commercial break, cutting off Darcy's rant.

As Alex turned down the radio, Laura did a fist pump in the air and said, "Yeah, girl."

Alex hadn't seen her get that animated in some time.

They looked at each other and laughed as Alex reached for the knob and turned off the radio.

"Wow," he said. "She's a bit of a pistol."

"I like it," said Laura.

"Me too. Kinda reminds me of someone else I know," Alex said as he looked at Laura and winked.

"Don't you forget it," said Laura in a playful voice as they pulled through the gates and drove up the long winding driveway toward the mansion.

Alex looked at Laura and said, "We can do this." He kissed her on the hand. "Welcome to our new adventure."

CHAPTER THIRTEEN

$\mathcal{I}$t had been one week since Alex, Laura, and Ben arrived home from the hospital. Alex had begun conducting interviews for a nanny and had seen at least a dozen applicants. He was not impressed with any of them. He was running on very little sleep and struggling to accomplish anything on the big account headed his way. At least he hoped it was headed his way.

Alex's boss, Mr. Hanson, put Alex and his team in charge of presenting their ideas for the new building to KYCL ownership, and the Landing firm was really counting on this account. That meant they were really counting on his team. Alex knew as team leader this could have a positive or negative effect on his career so he had to get this right.

The problem was, in order to give a presentation that was well thought out, precise, and organized, he had to be able to concentrate. He needed time to work and develop his ideas, and it had to be done soon. There was no time to waste. It was crunch time, and if he didn't solve this nanny crisis soon he was going to be in trouble. He had less than three months, and there was no way he was going to be ready if he didn't find some help.

What he really needed was for Laura to step up and start contributing some around the house. He needed her help, but he knew that wasn't a real option. He had been taking care of both her and Ben since they arrived home from the hospital.

Alex often found himself praying in moments of desperation. He felt guilty that he only seemed to go to God these days when he was in desperate need. Nonetheless, he prayed that morning as he drank his coffee.

"Please God, let me find some help today."

On the other side of town, Sara spent a few extra minutes that morning fixing her hair. She had a natural beauty about her, but she still always took the time to get herself looking perfect for the day.

She would laugh as she thought about what her dad used to say to her mom. He called her Beth, short for Elizabeth. He would always say, "Beth, you know you don't need makeup to be beautiful. Then again, every old barn looks better with a new coat of paint." He loved to tease her, and she loved every minute of it. That was one of Sara's favorite childhood memories.

As she was getting ready, Sara picked a professional looking dress that covered her knees, and she liked to wear a sweater with her outfit as well. Sara liked to dress modestly but did a good job of keeping up with the latest trends. She never wanted to be too showy. She liked to blend in.

Sara stopped by the bathroom one last time to brush her teeth and take a look in the mirror to make sure everything was acceptable, and then she proceeded to the door.

Sara lived in a downstairs basement apartment. The house was owned by Fred and Rita, an older couple who were so kind to her and let her live there for a good price. It was affordable, and in exchange Sara helped them out with some chores or cleaning when she could.

She knew she wouldn't stay here forever, but for now it was a great place to live. She grabbed her keys from the key holder hanging on the wall and headed out the door.

Rita was on the front porch as she drove out of the driveway in her dark blue 2010 Honda Accord. Sara stopped for just a second to say hello and wish Rita a good day.

"Good luck today with the job interview, child," Rita said. "We love you. I know you will be great. Just be yourself." Sara appreciated the encouragement, smiled, blew Rita a kiss, and headed for the freeway.

1730 Bunker Side Drive. The closer Sara got to the Maddox residence, the more she realized she was no longer in the small time. These neighborhoods were like something out of a movie. She found herself growing more and more nervous as the drive continued.

The GPS showed she was two point seven miles from her destination. Sara took a deep breath. Now, one point three miles away. Sara could feel her heart about to beat out of her chest. 700 feet.

"You have arrived at your destination," the GPS quoted.

Now the sweat was coming off her forehead. She was here. Sara pulled up to the gate and rang the intercom nervously and waited for the voice on the other side.

"May I help you?" a male voice asked.

"My name is Sara Patterson. I have a nine o'clock interview for the nanny position."

The gate opened slowly, and Sara drove down the drive toward what she thought had to be the biggest house she had ever seen in her life. As Sara turned off the car engine she looked toward the front door, and there stood one of the most handsome men she had ever seen outside of the movies.

She knew how nervous she got around ordinary people, and now she was going to have to sit through an interview with a Calvin Klein underwear model. She was now thinking this job opportunity just went from a long shot to impossible.

She took just a moment to gather her thoughts and reminded herself why she was here. She could do this. She could get this job and start working toward some of the goals she had been wanting to accomplish for so long now. She snickered for a moment as she said to herself, "I am interviewing to be a nanny, not a partner in a law firm."

But this was important to her, and she knew she was right where she was supposed to be and was going to make this interview count. Sara stepped out of the car with only her keys and her purse in her hands. She was trying to find the button on the key ring to lock the doors when she suddenly found herself crawling with horror as she accidentally hit the panic button, sending out a honking sound that was loud enough to wake the entire neighborhood.

She quickly turned off the alarm and gave Alex a gingerly "I'm sorry" wave and said to herself, "Good job, bonehead. You're off to a great start."

I don't know why I'm locking the doors anyway, Sara thought. *Well, I wouldn't want anyone stealing my nine-year-old Honda Accord in the middle of this million-dollar gated community.*

Trying to refocus on the task at hand, Sara turned toward the front door and dropped her keys on the driveway. After hastily bending down to pick them up, she stood back up and bumped her head on the mirror. She could feel the blood running from her cheeks, knowing that she was off to a bad start.

She heard a strong voice with a bit of a snicker say, "Well, that's using your head." She looked up, and there was Alex picking up her keys as he said, "I wish I had a quarter for every time I've done that."

He extended his hand and said, "Hello. I'm Alex Maddox, and you are Sara Patterson, I presume."

Sara nodded while giving Alex a timid hand shake.

"Well, I'm glad you're here," said Alex. "Let's head inside and talk about a few things." An unexpected calm came over Sara, and she knew she could do this. She just knew in her heart she would get this job.

CHAPTER FOURTEEN

*A*lex continued to make small talk with Sara as they approached the front door. As Sara entered the room, she couldn't help but comment on what a beautiful home they had. She immediately noticed the touch of a professional when it came to the interior design of the home. It was absolutely stunning, to say the least.

Alex showed Sara to the couch and invited her to have a seat. He offered Sara a tea or coffee. "That is, if I can figure out how to operate the Keurig."

"Tea would be great if it's not too much trouble," Sara said.

"I can do it," said Alex.

Sara sat gazing at the surroundings as Alex fumbled with the drinks.

He returned about three minutes later and said, "See, I knew I could do it."

"I never had a doubt," said Sara.

Alex sat across from Sara on the sofa with a bit of nervousness as Sara smiled back at him. "So Sara, how shall we begin?" Assuming Alex was about to begin, Sara waited quietly, but Alex looked at her and said, "No, seriously, I have no idea how to begin an interview."

"Well," said Sara, "If I were you I would say, 'So, Sara, tell me about yourself.'" Sara used a deep voice as if to imitate Alex. "And then you should ask me something about my strengths and weaknesses."

Alex laughed. "That's good," he said. "Let's start there."

Sara began to tell Alex about where she was born and raised, her relationship status, why she was here, what interested her about the job, and, of course, why she thought she would be a good nanny.

Sara then asked Alex if he could tell her a little about himself and his family. Alex cleared his throat and said, "Would you believe me if I told you we are actually pretty simple people?"

Sara laughed. "I'll take your word for it," she said.

Alex continued, "My wife, Laura, is an interior designer, and yes, as you can imagine, very successful and good at what she does. Hence the room you are looking at now. I know it looks fancy but we still prop our feet up and stretch out on the furniture around here."

Alex laughed as he pointed out that the furniture probably wouldn't be all that nice for long thanks to the arrival of Baby Ben. "I hear children have a way with furniture."

Sara laughed. "You are probably more right than you know."

Alex shifted gears as he told Sara a little about Laura and the past and some of the struggles they had faced. He shared about the upcoming job and how he seemed to be falling behind on everything. Suddenly Alex caught himself and apologized.

"I don't know why I am telling you all this," he said. "I guess it has just been a long time since someone has been interested and listened to me."

Sara felt a sudden calmness and assured Alex that it was good he was sharing with her. "I am planning on getting this job, which means I am going to be a part of your lives," she said. "I need to know something about you in order to be the best nanny possible for Ben."

Alex was impressed by Sara's confidence and the interest and initiative she was taking to get this position.

He wanted to stand up on the couch and jump for joy because he realized he had just found the help he had been looking for.

"Not to overstep or speak out of place," said Sara, "but can I be blunt with you for a moment?"

"Please do," said Alex. He was curious about what she had to say.

"You are obviously wealthy, and that affords you opportunities that many don't have," Sara said, noticing she now had Alex's full attention. "There is nothing wrong with that. It gives you the opportunity to help others. I don't know if you realize it, but by hiring me you are giving me a great gift, a great opportunity to be a part of something special."

"What are you getting at?" asked Alex.

"Well," said Sara, "I just think that after everything you have shared with me, you need much more than just a nanny. You need a staff to run this place. You need a cook, a maid, a groundskeeper, and yes, a nanny." As Alex was listening to what Sara was saying, he was liking the sound of everything he was hearing.

It would be nice to fill this home with people, Alex thought. *People who love what they do and want to be a part of a family.*

"I like it," said Alex. "You might be on to something here, and I think I might know just the person to make it happen."

"I'm going to need you to be available tomorrow morning, same time," he said excitedly. "Can you come back in the morning?"

"I'll be here," said Sara.

"Thank you so much," Alex said as he walked Sara to the door. "I'll see you in the morning, nine o'clock sharp."

CHAPTER FIFTEEN

*S*ara arrived at the front door of the Maddox residence at nine as scheduled. Alex wasted no time getting right down to business.

"You would be perfect," Alex said.

"I have no experience in running a household," said Sara.

"I have never hired anyone or even conducted an interview, but I know you are perfect," said Alex. "I'm going to need all of those positions filled that we have discussed, but without a house manager, it's not going to work.

"I need someone I can trust to oversee everything so that I can focus on my work, and I need to know that Laura and Ben are being cared for," he said. "It's going to be important that this household is run well because we are going to be in contact with prominent figures in the community. There will be times when we are hosting guests and being put in the public eye, and I need everything to run smoothly."

"So what would I be doing exactly?" asked Sara.

Alex smiled, "Does this mean what I think it means?"

"Yes, I'll take the job," Sara beamed. "Now, what exactly will I be doing?"

"You are going to be my house manager!

"First of all, let me tell you about your benefits package, and then I will explain to you your job responsibilities. Your salary for this position will be seventy-five thousand dollars, and you will be living in the guest house. I am setting you up with a car as well."

Sara thought this must be some kind of joke. She almost started to look around for the cameras to see if she was being pranked.

"How does the salary sound to you?" asked Alex.

"It's more than I ever dreamed of," said Sara.

"Make no mistake," said Alex, "This is going to be a real job with real responsibilities. Doing a great job can benefit you, and doing a poor job will get you fired.

"I have already shared with you a lot of personal information, and that is to be kept confidential."

"I understand," said Sara.

"There are going to be challenges that come with running this household, and I'm going to need you to be ready to handle them," Alex continued in a hurried and stern voice. "You will report directly to me, but the business of running the home will be entrusted to you."

Sara was beginning to feel a sense of both pride and fear all at the same time.

"I'd like you to start immediately," Alex commanded without really asking. "I will have a moving company get your things and get you set up in the guest house. Starting tomorrow, you are going to launch the hiring process to find a staff for this house."

Alex handed Sara a packet.

"I want you to review this. You are going to fill each of these positions and get the staff up and running. The packet explains how payroll will work, along with salaries and hours for the other positions.

"There is a full description of your job, and I hope it will answer any other questions you might have," he said. "You will be responsible for caring for Ben as well until you have filled the nanny position."

Alex pulled out all the official paperwork for hiring Sara.

"Let's do it," said Alex.

Sara began to fill out all the necessary paperwork and continued to ask a few questions as she went along.

Alex was glad to help her, and he was excited about the possibilities that his new employee was going to bring. He could almost feel the stress melting away by the minute. He knew he was making the right move. He just hoped Laura would feel the same. Then again, she didn't want to be a part of this process so she gave him free rein to do what he felt was best. She would have to live with the outcome, like it or not.

It was going on one o'clock when Sara handed Alex the last document and Alex extended his hand and said, "Congratulations, Ms. Patterson, you are my new house manager."

Pushing his hand aside, Sara leaned in for a hug and Alex squeezed her tight. Sara was squealing with excitement. Alex laughed.

"I'm so sorry," said Sara, "This is awesome."

"Don't apologize," Alex replied. "That's the enthusiasm I need."

Just then a look of horror came over Sara's face as she looked up and saw Laura coming down the stairs with a look that could cut right through a person.

"Laura, you're up," Alex said. "I want you to meet Sara. She is going to be helping us out around here."

"Was she your nine o'clock interview appointment?" asked Laura.

"Yes," said Alex.

"You do realize it is one o'clock, do you not?" Laura said sharply. "Was this a job interview or a date?"

Alex ignored Laura's biting comment and repeated the introduction. "Sara is going to be our new house manager."

"House manager, huh?" Laura snorted.

"Yeah," said Alex. "There are a few things I need to tell you about."

Sara extended her hand. "Laura, it's so nice to meet you."

"It's Mrs. Maddox," Laura said.

"Of course," Sara responded apologetically. "Thank you, Mrs. Maddox, for this wonderful opportunity."

Laura's confused look and fake "my pleasure" meant Alex would hear about this later, but he didn't care. He knew this was going to be a good thing.

"Let me walk you out," said Alex as he walked Sara to the door. "I want you to read the file tonight. I'll send the movers to your address, and I am planning on you being here on site no later than Friday. You will have the weekend to settle in, and Monday morning you will officially begin your work."

As Sara turned to leave, she was met by a blank stare from Laura.

She seems nice, Sara thought sarcastically as she walked toward her car.

CHAPTER SIXTEEN

*I*t had been a little more than two months since Sara started her new position with the Maddox family. It seemed like she had packed two years' worth of work into that small amount of time.

Sara found that she was pleased with the results so far, and she could see the difference it was making around the house.

Sara could tell that Alex was doing much better since he'd had the time to focus on his big upcoming account.

It was seven a.m., and Sara prepared to greet the staff on this lovely early November morning. She still couldn't believe that she was managing this household, and she took pride in thinking that she was definitely getting closer to her goals.

She loved the job and knew that she had exceeded all of Alex's expectations up to this point. She knew Laura didn't particularly care for her, but she had a feeling it would probably be that way with whoever Alex had hired. Sara was thankful that Laura kept to herself and let her do her job. It was unlikely Laura had the energy to deal with her anyway.

Laura wanted to get back to work but was struggling to find any new clients. Still, with all her idle time, she seemed so stressed. Laura did nothing but sleep, watch TV, or go to the spa.

How stressful can that be? Sara thought.

That was why Sara was there, along with Stella, Maggie, Louise the landscaper, Charlotte the chef, Emily the event planner, and of course Grace the nanny. Alex seemed pleased with all of her hires and had taken some time to get to know each of his employees. With the holidays coming, everyone was busy, and both Alex and Laura would need all the help they could get.

From what Sara could gather, Alex was giving his all to land the new big account at work. She could hear him talking with Laura in the evening sometimes.

It made her sad for Alex to see how little interest Laura took in what he did. Nonetheless, he did his best to keep Laura up to speed on what was going on in his life.

Sara wondered sometimes how Alex could stay so positive. She knew Laura was a beautiful woman, but she wished she knew if they were truly happy. Her hope was that maybe she could play some small role in making that happen.

They did take some time every evening to spend with Ben. It was kind of funny that they had a scheduled play time every evening after dinner. That was about all the time Ben ever got to see Alex and Laura even though Laura could spend more time with him if she wanted to.

One hour a day to invest in your son's life, Sara mused.

The rest of the time it seemed to be all on Grace. She was good at her job and seemed to genuinely care for Ben. She was the only other staff member that lived on the grounds full time. She had a room down the hall from Alex and Laura, right next to Ben.

Grace seemed to recognize and notice everything that was going on around the house.

"Alex and Laura do spend some time investing in one another during the evening, if you know what I mean," Grace said.

Sara didn't want to embarrass Grace, but she did have to talk to her about maintaining professionalism and remind her that gossip or sharing things that don't need to be shared could cost her the job. Grace said she understood and that she would do a better job of respecting the Maddoxes' privacy.

Sara realized now more than ever that this family could not function without the staff. They needed them as much as the staff needed their jobs, she thought.

Alex said he wanted this house to feel like a home, and with the addition of everyone working there and of course Grace and Sara living onsite, Sara thought the staff had definitely helped to accomplish that goal.

She thought more than anything that Alex just needed some kind of buffer from Laura. Of course, Alex would never say that directly to her, but Sara knew the longer she was here, the more she would learn about how deep his family problems were.

Sara thought about all those pleasant mornings she started her day off with a friendly conversation with Alex, only to have Laura walk in the room and completely change the whole mood.

Sara had just finished briefing the staff on the plans for the day, and everyone was off and running when the Maddoxes made an appearance.

As usual, Alex came down the stairs at seven thirty, but this time he was followed by Laura, much to everyone's surprise. She was never awake this early.

"Good morning, Mr. Maddox. Good morning, Mrs. Maddox," Sara said. Alex responded in kind but Laura never glanced Sara's way or said a word.

"Your breakfast orders are ready," Sara continued.

Alex and Laura stopped by the couch for a moment to say good morning to Grace and Ben, but mostly Ben. When they returned, Sara gave them the morning report and assured them that all staff members were accounted for and working hard.

Sara ran through the routine assessments and confirmed they still wanted dinner at 6:30 that evening.

"Yes, Sara," said Laura, answering for both of them. "That will be fine."

On this morning, Alex and Laura skipped breakfast and grabbed a coffee for the road. They changed so much from day to day, and they hardly ever came down at the same time. Nonetheless, it was Sara's job to keep it straight.

Some mornings Alex and Laura like to eat a bigger breakfast, some days a light breakfast, and some days just a coffee to go.

Sara always tried to find out the night before what they would want the next morning so she could coordinate with Charlotte, but many times they changed their minds at the last minute.

"I have messed up one breakfast order in the last two weeks," Sara mumbled to Charlotte, "and while Alex was forgiving, let me just say it won't happen again."

But on this particular morning, Alex grabbed his coffee and turned and gave Laura a big kiss, which she returned almost as if she were putting on a show for Sara's amusement.

"I'll see you tonight," Laura said. "Have a good day today."

"I will," said Alex. "You do the same."

"Goodbye, Sara," Alex said as he turned from Laura and smiled at Sara.

"Goodbye, Al — I mean, Mr. Maddox," she responded. "Have a great day."

Laura walked him to the door and kissed him one more time and closed the door behind her. Laura told Sara she would be out for the day as well. "I trust you have everything under control here."

"Yes, ma'am," Sara responded.

"If there is a problem, you are to call me," Laura said. "Do not bother Mr. Maddox for any reason."

"Yes, ma'am," Sara said as she handed Laura her coffee. "Have a great day, Mrs. Maddox."

Laura disappeared into the garage.

"You are to call me. Do not bother Mr. Maddox," Sara mumbled in a mocking voice. "Have a great day and don't come back, at least not until dinner tonight."

CHAPTER SEVENTEEN

*S*ara's hope came true. Laura spent the day at the spa and didn't return until five thirty that evening.

When Sara heard the garage door opening, she readied herself for her final performance of the day, as she always called it — dinner and a show.

Mrs. Maddox doesn't think I pay attention to her agenda, but I know more about what is going on around here than anyone, Sara thought as she took one more quick glance at the house and tidied a few more items on the kitchen counter.

A smiling Sara stood ready to greet the always disgruntled Mrs. Maddox as she walked through the kitchen door.

"Good evening, ma'am," Sara said with a burst of energy. "I hope you had a good day today."

"It would have been a good day if I could find someone to give me a decent massage," Laura replied.

"Well, everything went smoothly around here, and Charlotte is preparing you a wonderful dinner," Sara said without missing a beat. "She gets so excited about preparing your meals. She loves to cook and loves being here. We all love being here."

"Are you truly happy being in a servant's role?" Laura asked with a cutting edge.

"Oh, it's so much more than that," Sara replied. "I have a purpose here."

Laura spun around and chided Sara with a sharp, "I hope that purpose doesn't involve my husband."

"No, ma'am," Sara said, visibly upset. "I am so thankful for everything you and Mr. Maddox have done for me. I would never do anything to hurt your family."

"Okay, then. I just wanted to make sure we are clear on that," Laura said. "You wouldn't be the first. Girls have been trying to take him away from me since high school."

"Dinner will be ready in forty-five minutes," said Sara, shifting the subject quickly, "and then you have your family time with Ben and Alex this evening."

"Oh, yes. Family time," Laura said depressingly as she started up the stairs toward her room.

Watching Laura climb the stairs, Sara jumped when Alex slipped in and shifted his voice into a deep tone with, "What is happening in here?"

He was attempting to be funny but realized he truly startled Sara. "Are you okay?" he asked.

"Yes, yes, I'm fine. I'm sorry," Sara said. "I just didn't hear you come in. I'm a little overwhelmed with my to-do list this week, and I may have been focused on that."

"I know the feeling," Alex said, "but you are doing a great job."

"Mrs. Maddox is in the main bedroom if you would like to visit with her," Sara noted. "We're still planning on dinner at six thirty."

"Thank you, Sara. I'll see you in a little while," Alex said as he turned to walk away.

Turning around on his heels, Alex called back out to Sara.

"Yes, Alex?" Sara asked, noticing the softness in his eyes.

"I want to say thanks again for all you do," he said with a smile.

"You're welcome. Now go visit with your wife for a few minutes."

Sara let out a big sigh of relief that Alex hadn't heard any of her conversation with Laura. How awful that would have been. He had become such a good friend and a great boss. She didn't need anything messing this up now. She was right where she wanted to be and finally doing something she loved.

Alex and Laura came down for dinner right on time. "Perfect timing," said Sara, "and here comes Grace with Baby Ben."

Charlotte was busy helping everyone settle in while also preparing the plates. She did a basic cleanup of the kitchen before heading out while the family ate.

Grace would then clear the dishes and do the final cleaning after dinner so everything would be ready for breakfast the next morning.

All Alex and Laura had to do was focus on each other and Ben for the evening.

Sara wondered how hard that could be, but she knew the answer and it wasn't that simple. After the couple ate and exchanged pleasantries, Sara talked with Grace and made sure she was set for the night.

I have already said my goodbyes for the evening so when I finish with Grace, I can slip off to the guest house for my quiet evening, she thought.

Sometimes I wish I could be a fly on the wall for this part of the day. Maybe I should have the house bugged.

She chuckled and said goodnight to Grace. "Rest well," she told her.

"I will once I get that little fella to settle down," Grace said.

Sara laughed. "Good luck with that. Call me if you need anything. Otherwise, I'll see you in the morning." She slipped out the back door toward home.

CHAPTER EIGHTEEN

The day was finally winding down for Alex and Laura. It seemed like days ago since Alex had left for work that morning, yet there didn't seem to be enough work hours in the day to get everything done. If not for Sara and the rest of the staff, Alex knew he would not stand a chance.

Grace was getting Ben to sleep, and the game between the Knicks and the Jazz was about to tip off. Alex was hoping to settle in to watch some of the game. He rooted for the Jazz on most occasions, but he was still a Knicks fan at heart. He wondered which team Ben would cheer for. It didn't matter to Alex as long as he enjoyed the game. He broke into a big smile as he thought about taking his son to his first NBA game someday.

"What are you thinking about over there?" Laura asked.

"I was just thinking about how blessed we are," said Alex. "I hope we don't ever forget that."

"We do have it pretty good," Laura said as she returned to reading her *Cosmopolitan* magazine.

"Laura, was something wrong with Sara tonight?" asked Alex.

"What do you mean?" said Laura.

"Well, she just seemed rattled when I walked in the door, almost flustered, not her usual self."

"And what exactly is her usual self like?" asked Laura.

"Well, she's usually more enthusiastic," Alex responded. "She's happy, smiling, joking, usually excited to share the events of the day."

"Perhaps she doesn't have enough work to do if she is always happy, smiling, and joking," Laura said in a harsh tone.

"You know what I mean," said Alex. Alex could sense one of those moments where nothing was about to turn into something quickly, and he was not in the mood for any type of argument or confrontation, so why he said what came next, he would never know.

"Do you have some sort of problem with Sara?"

Laura dropped her magazine, looked up at him, and said, "Do I have a problem with a woman who lives in our guest house and has an obvious infatuation with my husband? Let me think for a minute."

"Come on," said Alex, "you know that is an outlandish statement. She does a great job around here, and yes, the job is different than what we had set out for originally, but you have to admit this household is running well."

"We are spending a fortune on help," Laura retorted.

"Help that we need," Alex fired back. "Plus, it's not like we can't afford it, and the reason we can afford it is because of our jobs and my trust fund. Without a proper staff I wouldn't even have the time to work on my accounts."

Laura rolled her eyes as he continued.

"And you said you were not going to be a stay-at-home mom. You don't like to cook. You don't like to clean. You're not going to do the yard work. You want your spa days, lunch meetings with friends, and what was the other thing? Oh yeah, work."

Alex knew he had hit a nerve with that one and wished he could take it back immediately. Laura had so many connections in New York and had a great portfolio, but she had not landed any big accounts since they moved to Salt Lake City. Most people would be willing to start small and work their way back up, but not Laura. She was not looking for just any job. She only wanted to work with big names and high-class clientele.

"I know you want to get back to work," Alex said in a kinder voice. "Something will come along. I know it will."

Laura just sat there quietly staring at her magazine.

"I do have some big news about my account at work," Alex said. "I would like to share it with you."

"Is it the radio station account?" Laura asked.

"Yes," said Alex. "I found out today that on Friday my team will be pitching a new building idea to the ownership of KYCL radio."

"The home of Darcy Campbell, Darcy Dishes It Out," added Laura.

"That's right," said Alex, "and Darcy is going to be a part of the meeting for our presentation."

Laura perked up. "She runs that station from what I understand, and because she brings all the listeners, the ownership wants her in on the new design. Everyone loves that woman," said Laura. "I've started listening to her quite a bit myself."

"I didn't know you were a Darcy groupie," said Alex, teasing Laura.

"Well, the woman has a good take on things, and I like the way she doesn't let any of those obnoxious callers push her around," Laura said.

"I think you would be a good radio host," said Alex. "No, make that a television host. You're too beautiful to be hidden away. You need to be in front of the camera for the world to see."

Laura playfully cut her eyes over at Alex, and the mood in the room quickly changed. Laura's demeanor softened as she moved in closer to Alex. Alex loved these moments because they reminded him of why he loved Laura so much. He just wished they were not so few and far between.

As Alex and Laura made love, Grace was down the hall watching over Ben. She cranked up her headphones to block out the noise. Laura then fell fast asleep, and Alex lay there watching the game until he eventually drifted off to sleep.

The next morning when Laura woke up, Alex had already headed downstairs where Charlotte had prepared some oatmeal and muffins as requested. Everything was beautiful as usual. A few minutes later, Laura came down the stairs to find Alex greeting Sara at the back door as she arrived at her usual time and ready to discuss the day's agenda with Alex. They always had to make sure that everyone was on the same page for the day's activities.

"Good morning," said Laura in a low tone.

"Good morning, Mrs. Maddox," said Sara.

Laura was thinking how Sara was always there, always right there. She knew Sara was necessary though, and so she didn't fight Alex on his hiring of her. Laura ate some breakfast as she listened in on Alex and Sara discussing the agenda for the day.

Suddenly Alex said, "I have to get going," and headed for the door.

Laura jumped up and walked Alex to the door and started to kiss him goodbye when Sara called out, "Good luck getting ready for tomorrow's big account pitch, Mr. Maddox."

Immediately Laura's mood shifted, and tension suffocated the room as Laura pulled away from Alex and said, "How does she know about the account?"

"I told her," said Alex.

"When?" Laura asked. "I just found out myself last night."

"I told her when I got home yesterday. She asked me how my day was and I told her. I was excited, and I wanted to share the news."

"Is there anything else the hired help knows about that you haven't shared with your wife yet?" Laura asked.

Alex leaned in and said in a calm voice, "You know that's not fair." When Laura gave him an ugly look, he added, "You're not interested half the time anyway."

Laura stood there looking disgusted.

"I don't want to start my day this way. Please forgive me," said Alex as he kissed Laura on the cheek and headed out the door.

Sara had already left the room and was fast getting to work so she wouldn't catch any more grief than necessary from Laura. Laura headed up the stairs, and Sara was thankful that was all she had to see of her until dinner later that night.

CHAPTER NINETEEN

*A*lex was not in the best of moods after his little confrontation with Laura that morning. It was a confrontation that was not necessary in the first place. He had more important things to be dealing with and did not need to be distracted with any extra drama. It was approximately a twenty-minute drive to the office, and traffic seemed to be flowing well this morning. Alex was beginning to relax and clear his head. As he was just about to turn on to the freeway, he looked up and there was Darcy's bigger-than-life billboard.

I think the advertising department knew what they were doing when they put her picture up for all the world to see, he thought. *She is a beautiful woman.*

Alex was surprised the billboard didn't cause more wrecks from people staring. Alex started to get eager about meeting her the next day. About that time, Alex's phone was ringing. Alex didn't usually answer his phone unless it was work, so he picked it up to hear the voice of his boss speaking with an urgency he knew couldn't be good.

"What is it, Mr. Peterson?" Alex asked.

Mr. Peterson didn't take a breath as he spouted out in a panic, "The meeting with KYCL, they want to meet today. They have us scheduled for an eleven o'clock lunch meeting at the Grand. They ended up with some conflicts and need to meet today. We need to take them up on it; otherwise we might not have the opportunity to pitch our idea to the owners of the station."

"I'm on my way in now," said Alex. "I'll be there by eight thirty."

When Alex hung up the phone with Mr. Peterson, he immediately called Wanda, his secretary. He explained the situation quickly and said he needed the team assembled in the board room ASAP. The next two hours were a blur as the team put the finishing touches on the presentation. They were out the door by ten forty and headed to the Grand to meet with Mr. Pascal, the owner of KYCL; Mr. Terry, the head of management for the station; and Darcy Campbell, the most popular on-air talent in the tri-state area.

The team arrived at the restaurant and was escorted to the Colonial room at the Grand. It was a private room for exclusive business meetings, and it had all of the technology and comforts they needed for their presentation. Shortly after Alex, his team, and Mr. Peterson arrived at the Grand, they were set up and ready to go, and not a minute too soon. As the door to the Colonial room opened, Alex saw a short bald man, followed by a slightly taller middle-aged man, followed by none other than Darcy Campbell. Alex was absolutely blown away. He could feel the sweat starting to pour off of his forehead. But he calmly stepped forward and introduced himself to each member of the KYCL team and then introduced his boss and his team members.

Darcy spoke first. "We are really excited to see what you're going to present to us today. I've been trying to talk Pascal there into loosening the purse strings for years now. It's about time we updated the place." Everyone in the room except Mr. Pascal laughed.

"Don't mind him," said Darcy. "He's a teddy bear."

Alex laughed and said, "Let me show each of you to your seats."

Darcy liked the way Alex took charge of the room. After everyone was seated, Alex said, "I am aware of your schedules, and we're going to be considerate of your time. Is anyone else hungry?"

Everyone was hesitant to answer until Darcy said, "I could eat an elephant right now."

"Great. Let's eat before we get down to business," Alex said. "I will plan on giving you the presentation at about noon. It will only last about thirty minutes. That will give you time to ask some questions and get back to the radio station for your show at two. How does that sound?"

"Sounds great," said Darcy. It was as if no one else was even in the room.

"I find it's hard to concentrate when I'm starving," said Alex.

"Yeah," said Darcy, "or when the person next to you has a stomach that is growling so loudly that you can't even hear the presentation."

"Very funny," said Pascal.

Over the next hour, the group got to know a little about one another as they enjoyed a wonderful lunch. When everyone had finished dessert and was settling in with their coffee, Alex said, "Well, now for the fun part."

For the next thirty minutes, Alex made a presentation that dazzled everyone in the room. He was both knowledgeable and funny. He kept the audience involved and had them eating out of his hand.

When he finished, Mr. Pascal and Darcy asked if they could have the room for a few minutes.

After about five minutes of discussion, they called Alex and his team back in and told Mr. Peterson and company that the Landing would be the official architectural firm for this project.

After many handshakes and congratulations, Darcy grabbed Alex by the arm and said she needed to speak with him for a moment.

"Certainly," said Alex. He could tell the tone in her voice had changed, and he was hoping it was nothing too serious as they walked to the private patio connected to the Colonial room.

CHAPTER TWENTY

*A*s Alex closed the patio door, Darcy said, "Alex, I want you to know that I think your presentation was absolutely brilliant. I like the way you take charge. I like the way you are considerate of our time. I like that you wanted to eat and do a little socializing before we talked business. I've got a really good feeling about you."

"Thank you," said Alex, "but I'm afraid you're about to give me some bad news."

"Well, not so much bad news as a heads up. Mr. Pascal was impressed with you, but you were not his first choice. I went to bat for you because I believe in you. I just need you to assure me that you can deliver to us exactly what you are promising."

"I can," said Alex. "The presentation that I showed you today is just the beginning. When you see the real thing, you are going to know that you made the right decision. I promise you, Darcy, you have nothing to worry about. You are in good hands. Your station is in good hands."

"I know you have to get going, but I actually wanted to ask you about something as well," Alex said in a serious voice.

"Okay," said Darcy. "What is it?"

"Well, I was wondering if you would be interested in attending my family's Christmas party this year, and by you I mean KYCL. I would like to host your entire station. It's kind of a tradition my wife and I have, and being new here, we don't have that many friends yet. I know Laura would love to host your station along with my work colleagues this year for our party."

"I think that's a fabulous idea," said Darcy. "You are talking about a lot of people."

"We can handle it," said Alex. "It will be fun. Maddox Christmas parties are legendary."

"I can't wait," said Darcy. "We will be there. I think this could go a long way toward winning over Mr. Pascal as well. If you host a party, he won't have to. You save that man any money at all, and he will be your best friend," she said with a laugh. "Is this something you can afford? I'm not trying to sound insulting; I just want to make sure you are certain."

"I'll be fine," said Alex. "Legendary, I promise."

Darcy laughed as she asked, "And you are certain Laura will have no problem with this?"

"My wife loves to throw parties. She's a very talented interior designer and is always complaining that not enough people get to see her work."

"Interior design, you say? I might have to pick her brain," said Darcy.

"That would be great," said Alex. Alex knew right then and there that he was a dead man, but hopefully with Laura getting the chance to meet Darcy and maybe even get a job out of it, Alex might live to see another day.

"I look forward to meeting your family," said Darcy, "and I'm excited about the opportunity to get to know you better as this process continues." Darcy surprised Alex by giving him a hug before heading for the door. "Thanks for everything, Alex. I'll see you soon."

Alex stood there speechless. He wasn't quite sure what he had just gotten himself into.

CHAPTER TWENTY-ONE

*A*lex couldn't believe December twenty-third was here. He had spent the last several weeks working closely with Darcy and the rest of the management team from KYCL, so they would be ready to break ground on the new building sometime in January. As Alex sat in his study looking at the specs for the project, he heard Laura call to him from the living room.

"I know you are not in there working when we're only two hours away from hosting almost three hundred people I don't even know," she chided jokingly but nervously.

"It's going to be fine," Alex responded. "The staff has done a wonderful job getting ready, and everything is beautiful. Darcy can't wait to meet you, and I am certain when she sees the beautiful job you have done with our home and the tree and the decorations, she will most likely offer you a job." That made Laura smile.

Just then Sara peeked her head in the room and said, "Mr. Maddox, what were you thinking?" Alex looked at Sara with a sort of dazed stare. "Three hundred people? I don't even know three hundred people."

"Thank you, Sara," said Laura as she joined her at the door and both stared at Alex. Alex had to admit he felt a little ganged up on, but it was nice to see Laura and Sara agreeing on something for once.

After a few seconds of staring at Alex with a quirky smile, Laura turned to Sara with the most sincere look Sara had ever witnessed. "I think you have done a wonderful job," Laura told Sara. "I think everything looks perfect."

Sara, taken aback a bit, brushed off the compliment. "Emily is the one to thank. She is good at her job," Sara said. "I'm so glad she's a part of our staff, and Charlotte has a menu planned that is fit for kings and queens. The house is spotless. Louise has the yard in perfect condition and decorated beautifully. All kidding aside, tonight is going to be great."

The three of them all shook their heads in agreement, and then Sara turned back into commander mode, looked at both Alex and Laura, and said, "Now, I need the two of you to go and finish getting ready. I've got you covered, I promise."

And she did. Sara had the entire household running like clockwork. Grace was in the playroom with Ben dancing to some Christmas tunes. You could hear him giggle and knew he was having fun. All was well in the Maddox household for the moment.

As seven thirty neared and the first guests arrived, Alex and Laura were filled with a sense of anticipation about what the evening might bring. They greeted each person in a way that made them feel like royalty, but they both knew in the back of their minds they couldn't wait for the arrival of one Ms. Darcy Campbell. It was about three minutes after eight when Darcy and her entourage pulled up to the house. You could feel the excitement in the air. As Darcy approached the door, Laura was the first to introduce herself.

"Ms. Campbell, it is truly a pleasure."

"Well, first of all, it's Darcy. Ms. Campbell is my mom, and the pleasure is mine," Darcy said. "Your husband is so talented, and we have been truly blessed to have him working on our new building."

Laura was a little jealous that Darcy was bragging on Alex, but her mood changed quickly when Darcy said, "And I hear you are quite the interior designer."

"I try," Laura responded sheepishly.

"Well, from the looks of your beautiful home I would say you are quite talented," Darcy said while peering through the door into the house. "Alex has been so excited for me to see your home and what you have done with the place. It doesn't disappoint."

"Thank you," said Laura. "We truly are honored to have you and your station here tonight. Did you bring a date," asked Laura, "or are you flying solo?"

"I like to fly solo," said Darcy. "I don't want to be tied down in case I meet Mr. Right tonight. You never know where these parties will lead, and I like to keep my options open."

A few of the young men in the room who were eavesdropping perked up a little when they heard that, but the comment took Alex back a little bit. He brushed it off because he was focused on Laura tonight. She was lighting up the room in spectacular fashion. Alex could see the guys from the station and his work as well checking out his wife. He couldn't blame them. She was a hottie. This was the most proud he had been of her in a long time.

Staring at Laura with a grin on his face, Alex was snapped back to the present when Darcy roped her arm around his.

"Laura, I apologize. I know this is a party but I need to borrow your handsome husband for just a few minutes before we dive into the fun for the evening," Darcy said as she pulled him away from Laura's side.

"Certainly," Laura said with a bit of hesitation. She was more comfortable with Alex by her side, especially with how handsome he looked in his tuxedo. But Laura went back to focusing on the guests as Alex and Darcy slipped off into the study for what seemed like an eternity to Laura, but in reality was only about five minutes.

"I won't keep you long," said Darcy, "but I need you to make the adjustment to the cubicle in section 4c on the specs."

"I know the one you're talking about," Alex said as he unfolded the plans across his desk, pushing his keys out of the way to make room. The key ring caught Darcy's eye as it slid across the surface. "Luke 8:17. What is that all about?" asked Darcy.

"It is a reminder from my mother to always stay out of trouble," Alex said a little sheepishly. Darcy snickered. "It's a long story," he said, changing the subject back to what Darcy needed to talk about.

"Mr. Pascal is looking for everything to be finalized, and he will be a bit of a pain until it gets done," Darcy continued. Rambling on about Mr. Pascal, Darcy circled Alex's study admiring the various trinkets and books. Suddenly she stopped talking and stared at the glass casing on the far side of the room. Fascinated, she walked over and looked closely at the intricate details of the gun inside the case. She really wanted to hold it but refrained from asking.

"I never took you for the shoot 'em up kind," she said, teasing him. Alex laughed. "I am not opposed to guns, but I am certainly not the shoot 'em up kind. That gun there is a Colt 1851 Navy Revolver," Alex said with some swagger. "It belonged to my grandad. He was a great man. I really miss him."

"I'm sorry," said Darcy. "I didn't mean to get off task."

"That's OK," said Alex.

Switching gears, Darcy said, "After tonight I'll be leaving to spend some time in Aspen for a few days with my family at our cabin. I will be gone until after the New Year but when I return, we will have a few final meetings and it will be go time. The deadline is approaching quickly."

"I'm on it," Alex said. "Anything else?"

"Yes," said Darcy, "Just one more question."

"What is it?" asked Alex.

"Why is there a mistletoe hanging in your study?"

Alex turned red and couldn't find a response.

"Relax," said Darcy, "This is a party, Silly. I will be expecting a dance a little later, Mr. Maddox."

"You bet," said Alex. "I have some pretty good moves."

"Can't wait," said Darcy with a giggle. As Alex opened the door to the study, he had his hand on Darcy's back and was escorting her out the door when they were met by Laura almost immediately.

"I was getting worried," Laura said.

"We're finished," said Darcy. "Let's get this party started."

CHAPTER TWENTY-TWO

*L*ater that evening as the party started to die down a little, Darcy walked over and sat down next to Laura on the couch. Laura was a little suspicious of Darcy and the certain fondness she seemed to have for her husband, but she quickly warmed up when Darcy started to talk interior design.

"I want to know a little about your design experience," said Darcy. "I love the decor in this place."

"Well, I'm a Syracuse graduate," Laura replied.

"I won't hold that against you," Darcy interrupted with a smile while slapping her on the leg.

Laura forced a smile in return and continued. "Of course, interior design was my major, but I grew up around the business. My mom is very talented. She has helped me a lot." Laura went on to mention some of the bigger clients she had in New York.

Impressed with Laura's résumé, Darcy shared why she was so interested.

"I'm in the process of moving into my new home in the Hill area," she said. "It's a bit more than I need, but the station wants me to look as high profile as possible so I'm upgrading. I'm going to need that place decorated, and it's going to have to look good. Would you be interested in throwing some ideas my way, and let's see if we can't work you into getting me set up? It will be a big job if you're up for it."

"I would love to," said Laura. "When can we start?"

Darcy could see the look of enthusiasm on Laura's face so she hated to tell her they would have to wait until after the New Year. "I will be out of town at my family's ski lodge in Aspen until a few days after the New Year. If you're flexible, I'll have my assistant set up a time for us to meet when I return."

"That sounds great," said Laura. "I'll be looking forward to it."

It had been so long since Laura had a big job opportunity come her way that she had to remind herself to remain professional and not jump up on the couch and start celebrating. Refocusing and redirecting the conversation back to Darcy, Laura asked, "What does the radio station do while you're gone?"

"Oh, they'll be fine. They run the best of Darcy Dishes It Out for a couple of weeks. The listeners tend to enjoy it, and it gives me a chance to get away, relax, and get in some skiing."

The evening was starting to wind down, but the staff stayed busy tending to everyone's needs, and the laughter and flirting in the room remained in high gear. Finally, at about one a.m., Darcy said, "Okay, people. Out." When Darcy spoke, people listened. Darcy took a minute to tell Laura goodbye, told her she couldn't wait to start on their project, and gave her a big hug. She then walked over to Alex and gave him a big hug followed by a kiss on the cheek and thanked him for being such a wonderful host.

"I will see you soon," said Alex. "Have fun skiing."

Darcy winked at Alex and turned to Laura with a quick wave as she said, "You are a lucky girl. Merry Christmas, everyone."

As Darcy made her exit, all the other guests scurried out behind her and the clean-up crew kicked into motion.

"I'm exhausted," said Laura. "I'm headed off to bed. Alex, will you be joining me?"

"Yes, dear. I'll be up in a minute," he said. Alex took a moment to go over a few things with Sara and thanked her for her hard work. Sara knew that by the time Alex and Laura woke up for breakfast in the morning, there would be no hint that a party with more than three hundred people had even taken place the night before.

"Get some rest," Sara told Alex. "We've got it all covered. By the way, I think tonight was a big success." Alex started for the stairs when Sara called him back. "I'm sorry. I almost forgot this envelope is for you. In all the hustle, I forgot to give it to you."

"What is it?" Alex asked.

"I'm not sure," Sara replied. "It's from Darcy. She just asked me to make sure that you received it. She said it was important to the account and you would understand what it meant."

"Thank you, Sara," said Alex. "And great job tonight."

CHAPTER TWENTY-THREE

*A*lex and Laura both slept solidly that night. Laura woke up excited about their quiet Christmas Eve and Christmas Day plans at home and that Trevor and Michele were coming to visit for New Year's. They would be arriving on the twenty-seventh and staying for the entire week. It would be the first opportunity for their kids to meet. Alex hadn't seen Laura this animated in years. With the prospect of Laura having a job opportunity with Darcy Campbell along with watching Laura come out of her shell, Alex was beginning to think that moving out West was the right thing to do. The new year was shaping up to be a great year!

As Alex was sitting in his study thinking about all that was going on, he remembered the envelope Sara had given him from Darcy. He opened the envelope, pulled out a folded letter and began to read.

"Alex, I have had so much fun getting to know you over the past few weeks. I find myself smiling every time I think about you. I would like it if you would text me over the holidays. I know we still have several business meetings and I will get to see you when I get back, but I don't want to wait that long to hear from you. I am giving you my private number. My number is 314-645-8976. I look forward to hearing from you. Don't make me wait too long. —DC"

Alex picked up his phone and put Darcy's number into his contacts under the name Johnny Stone. Johnny was an intern at the Landing and Alex would never need to call him, but his name was a good cover for the time being.

He sat there for a moment thinking of what he should say to her, and then the reality of the situation hit him. This was not right, and he knew as a married man, he should not be contacting this woman for any reason outside of business. Alex put his phone away and started for the living room where he found Laura sitting and playing with Ben.

"Look at you two," Alex said.

"Come join us, Daddy," Laura said in a playful voice. "We have your Christmas present ready for you."

As Alex and Laura sat there playing with Ben, Alex tried to act excited about the special platinum desk plaque with Ben's hand and feet prints but was distracted by the note he had just read. He couldn't stop thinking about Darcy and what she had written. Alex heard Laura's voice in the background of his daydreaming but wasn't really paying attention until he heard, "Hello, Alex. Anybody home?"

"Hey, Sweetie," said Alex. "I'm fine, just a little distracted with everything that's going on and worried at how long it's taking for Sara to finalize your gift. But never mind that. I'm just glad to be here with my two favorite people."

"Oh, and I think one of them needs to be changed," he said with his nose scrunched up.

As Grace grabbed Ben, Laura mentioned again how excited she was that Trevor and Michelle were coming to visit.

"They will be here in just three days. I can't believe it," she said. "It is going to be so much fun. We have so much to catch up on."

CHAPTER TWENTY-FOUR

*I*t was a little rainy and a bit foggy outside, but in Laura's mind it was a beautiful day. Trevor, Michelle, and the kids would be arriving at the house at about eleven, so Laura and Alex tried to pass the final hour away before their arrival by tidying up the house, still somewhat of a toy disaster zone following Christmas morning.

When the doorbell rang at five after, Laura headed toward the foyer yelling out, "I've got it."

"Not if I get there first," Alex screeched as he ran past her to fling open the door.

As soon as Alex opened the door, Trevor, without missing a beat, said, "How's it going, Ugly?" as he pushed his way past Alex to give Laura a big hug.

"Yep, nothing has changed," said Michelle as she laughed and hugged Alex.

Alex and Laura introduced Baby Ben to Ashley and Katelyn, who were so excited to get to play with a baby. And Laura couldn't believe how tall the girls were.

About that time Trevor caught a glimpse of Sara, who had walked through the back door.

"What, do you just have models coming and going now as they please?" he asked Alex. "Is your beautiful wife not enough to look at?"

"No, Dummy," Alex responded, punching Trevor on the arm. "This is Sara. She is our house manager."

"House manager, you say? Nicely done," Trevor said in a sleazy voice, garnering laughter from Alex and Michelle but not Laura. She was not amused but didn't let it get to her because she knew that was just how Trevor was.

In the few minutes it took Laura to flag down Grace to take the kids to the playroom for some snacks and games, Trevor had already launched into a deep conversation with Sara.

But Laura was determined not to share her friends — not on this visit — so she pulled him away and offered to give Trevor and Michelle a tour of the house. The next hour flew by as the four friends talked nonstop, catching up on every aspect of all their lives.

Grace could barely get their attention to let them know lunch was ready. And when they turned to head to the dining room, Trevor asked Grace if she would be joining them.

"The help does not eat with us," Laura inserted sharply and quickly. And a heavy tension crept all around the room.

Michelle diverted everyone's attention by asking what was on the menu and noting how wonderful it sounded.

Lunch extended into the afternoon as the conversation picked up, but finally the guys decided to break away for some one-on-one time. They settled into Alex's study while the ladies went to check on the kids. Laura also wanted to show off her Christmas gift from Alex, a Buccio Tuscany Italian leather briefcase with an engraved 14-karat gold plate showcasing Philippians 4:13.

"I was a little surprised Alex chose a Bible verse instead of my initials," Laura said, "but I thought it was sweet he remembered my favorite Scripture from when we were young: 'I can do all things through Christ who strengthens me.'"

Michelle quickly grabbed the briefcase, clicked the shoulder strap in place and tossed it over her shoulder. "Bradbury, please bring the car around," she said in a sultry, elitist-style voice while prancing around with her nose in the air. Laura laughed so loud it startled Alex as he closed the door to the study.

"So what's really going on in the Maddox household?" Trevor asked Alex point-blank. "And don't tell me the boring stuff. I want to know how you and Laura really are."

"There is something interesting going on around here," said Alex, "and against my better judgment I am going to share it with you."

"Lay it on me," Trevor said, rubbing his hands together with excitement as Alex told Trevor about the note.

"Is this the girl you were telling me about?" Trevor asked.

"I'm sure you saw her picture on a couple of billboards on your way in," Alex said.

"Oh, yeah. Michelle even slapped me one time when I commented how beautiful she was," Trevor said. "So how did this happen?"

Alex told Trevor as much as he knew — and how it was making him feel — right up to the Christmas party and then stopped. "What do I do now?" he asked.

Trevor pretended to contemplate the options and then said with all seriousness, "There is only one thing to do."

"Okay. What?" Alex asked.

"We have to text Darcy," Trevor said with that familiar mischievous look in his eyes.

"I'm serious," Alex said.

"So am I," Trevor shot back. "Let's have some fun with it. What's the big deal?"

It was nothing new for Trevor to encourage Alex to do something crazy "and just have some fun," but this was not some high school prank. This was Alex's job and his marriage they were talking about. Alex was angry at himself for even telling Trevor about the note in the first place, but he did and now he was beginning to be more intrigued himself. Meanwhile, Trevor was slowly giving him the confidence to do the exact thing he knew he shouldn't do but wanted to — text Darcy.

Alex picked up his phone, went to his contacts, and punched the number for Johnny Stone.

"Hey, Darcy. It's Alex. Wanted to check on you."

As Alex and Trevor sat there acting like two middle school boys trying to get up the courage to ask a girl to dance, Alex's phone made a bing.

"I was wondering if I was going to hear from you," the text read. "Took you long enough."

Alex knew he had started down a dangerous path and for a minute he wanted to take it back, but against all of his better judgment he continued down this road that was surely not going to lead anywhere good.

CHAPTER TWENTY-FIVE

*T*he new year was up and running with all the hustle and bustle of the holidays finally quiet. Alex was in day ten of his constant text conversation with Darcy, and she had arrived back in town two days ago. The only time he couldn't get a response from her was when she was on the air. They talked about everything. It was as if he had known her his whole life. He found that he could not wait to tell her how his day unfolded.

Darcy was interested in knowing everything, from how his checkup at the doctor went to if he won his pickup basketball game at the YMCA. There also was the constant flirting and fun little ego-boosting comments she made that he loved so much. And he gave as good as he got when it came to the constant barrage of compliments and flirtatious innuendos.

Alex found himself really wanting more and fantasizing about a weekend getaway, a chance to escape everything and just be with her for a couple of days.

But Darcy's celebrity status made any type of time together outside of their business meetings almost impossible. The challenge would be making sure TMZ reporters didn't catch some sound bite for their nine thirty evening broadcast.

The paparazzi wasn't Alex's only concern, however. Along with the obvious fact that everything going through Alex's mind was straight-up wrong and inappropriate — after all, Laura was his wife and he made a commitment before her and God that he would remain faithful to her — Alex also knew his work was suffering because of his obsession with Darcy.

He also found himself jealous of Laura because her new role as Darcy's interior designer meant she would get to spend time with Darcy almost every day.

What's wrong with me? Alex thought, pacing around the room. *Not only should I not be talking to Darcy like this, but I'm doing it with Laura right there in the room with her. Wow, I'm playing a risky game, and it's kind of strange too.*

Alex's mind shifted back to Darcy and determined it was worth the risk. *If it doesn't bother Darcy, then I'm not going to worry about it either,* he thought. *Apparently Darcy wants this as much as I do, and she obviously keeps her phone secure.*

About the time he thought about Darcy's phone, his phone reminder notice went off and almost made him stumble as it shook him out of his daydream.

Back to work, he thought, as he centered himself for the conference call meeting that would capture the next few hours. "Remember you have a job to do," Alex said as punched himself on the leg, "and a well-paying job at that."

But his mind wandered off again because of the conference call. He had been on several conference calls with Darcy and the management of KYCL, and it took everything he had in him to focus as she talked. He really wished he could have met with her in person rather than on the phone — and he knew she felt exactly the same way. He felt the connection and sensed the same desire coming from her that burned inside him.

Yes, we both talked about the project and kept the conversation all business, but we definitely both had other business on our minds, he almost said out loud but then caught himself. *We've done so well hiding our feelings for each other from all of those around us, I'd better get my act together before I mess this up.*

Scanning the final KYCL draft changes and attaching the file, Alex hit send on the email and then pulled the file for the conference call coming in from the law firm in two minutes ... no make that one minute ... ring, ring. "Hello, Mr. Beasley."

CHAPTER TWENTY-SIX

*L*aura absolutely loved working on the interior design plan for Darcy's new home. She popped up each morning ready to go. She had an energy she had not experienced in a while.

Along with the fulfillment she received from the work itself, Laura enjoyed the friendship developing between her and Darcy even more.

Bouncing through the door just in time for dinner, Laura was chatting on the phone with Darcy.

Alex wondered if she hadn't had enough time with Darcy already today. Still, he couldn't help but smile as he noticed the excitement in Laura's voice and spirit.

"I thought our house was big," he heard Laura say. "But your house is a castle, and I'm going to make it fit for a queen," she said with a giggle as she wrapped up the conversation.

Alex wasn't sure how Laura segued so easily, but she said goodbye to Darcy in one breath and transitioned the conversation straight to him. It was as if he had been part of the original dialogue.

"Darcy says she doesn't really need a place that large, but it's about image," Laura said matter-of-factly to Alex. "You know, she needs to do everything she can to keep up the proper appearances, and I definitely understand. It makes sense and after all …"

Laura's voice faded into a muffle as Alex's mind wandered to his own desire to talk about and with Darcy. *We never have enough time to talk through our texts,* Alex thought as his mind shifted farther and farther away. He snapped back to reality when he heard Laura saying, "Alex, Alex, earth to Alex."

Regaining eye contact with Laura, he apologized and made up an excuse about being hungry and thinking about how the meal on the table was getting cold.

"Oh, of course. Silly me," Laura said. "Let's get ready for dinner. I can finish the story while we eat."

Laura could fill the entire dinnertime conversation with her stories these days, and she loved sharing every detail with Alex. This was something she had not wanted to do for a really long time now.

And while Alex knew he should be overjoyed about Laura's consistent good mood and interest in sharing with him, he barely listened as she talked. For so long the evenings were filled with silence, and now there was an endless giddy chatter, but Alex remained dissatisfied.

He knew Darcy was only a fantasy and Laura was his reality, so he should do everything he could to focus on Laura.

It was a losing battle for the time being. He could hardly concentrate on what Laura was saying. He feigned interest in her day and what she wanted to share. He smiled and nodded and occasionally mumbled "uh-huh" and "that's great" and other generic references when she took a breath.

All the while, his patience level was maxed out. It was all he could do not to run to the study to settle in to an evening of texting with Darcy. *Family time never lasts this long*, he thought, still forcing out the cheesy smile.

Alex reminded himself that it was almost Laura's bedtime. *Hang in there*, he told himself.

Laura didn't mind Alex working after family time these days. She understood that big accounts need extra attention and was grateful he was willing to schedule some time with her and Ben.

Besides, Laura was putting in some heavy hours herself working on design plans and fabrics for Darcy's new home. It actually helped Laura to have some time to work as well in the evening. Laura didn't have to feel bad if Alex was busy with his accounts.

As both Alex and Laura thought through what they would work on as soon as they wrapped up their time with Ben, they also played and acted like they were totally present in the moment. They both had gotten good at faking in times like these.

I'm the only one who knows the struggle I am facing right now, Alex thought. *I am working hard, but it's definitely not all work. I do make sure I have my time in the evenings to talk with Darcy, and I love how she always makes time to talk with me.*

Trevor often texted Alex to ask the latest on the Darcy saga, and Alex always assured him that he had not contacted her anymore, nor would he. Trevor didn't buy it and pushed hard to try to trip Alex up with his stories.

Alex straight up lied to Trevor and never blinked about it. In fact, lying was coming all too easily to Alex now. He even prided himself on how good he'd gotten at it.

"Lord knows I'm getting a lot of practice at being deceitful," Alex almost said out loud as he felt a twinge of guilt.

He was pulling his phone out of his pocket to see if by chance he had a message from Darcy, but Laura was nearby. *Whoa, what am I doing?* Alex thought. *I have to stop. I don't need to throw any more fuel on the fire than I already have.*

So why am I sitting here still waiting on the next text from Darcy? A woman he didn't see outside of business meetings had him tied up in knots.

Saying goodnight to Laura and Ben, Alex strolled down the hall to his study and got lost in the evening's conversation.

But there was that small voice in Alex's head that kept prodding him to turn and run away. If only he would listen.

Alex continued to justify his actions and the path he was now following even though he knew down deep it was absolutely and totally wrong. He also found himself resenting Laura more and more. Why? She wasn't the one stepping over the line. But for some reason it would be easier if he could find reasons to blame her.

Alex knew he was growing more and more distant from Laura with each passing day and was starting to lose focus on his work. He realized that he couldn't concentrate on anything except his fantasy relationship with Darcy.

It was truly starting to consume Alex.

Alex texted Darcy and told her that he had to see her. Darcy responded that she wouldn't be able to see him until their scheduled meeting next Monday.

Alex insisted that was not good enough.

"Please find a way to meet with me," he begged.

"I wish I could but I just can't right now."

She even went on to outline an entire list of meetings and events to prove she was telling the truth.

She told Alex as she had so many times before that she was not in this to destroy his marriage. She just enjoyed the conversation of "a very interesting and handsome man."

Darcy assured Alex things could be different if he were not with Laura anymore, but Alex explained that it wasn't an option.

And the dance continued.

Darcy gave Alex a choice.

"We can either continue to have some innocent fun without having to be so secretive, or we can be done with this. It's up to you.

"This is not easy for me either," Darcy told Alex. "But that is just the way it has to be."

"I love you. Goodbye for now," was Darcy's final text of the night, followed by a picture of her in a beautiful red dress.

Alex knew he was in the deep end of the pool and in desperate need of being rescued.

The question in his mind was, did he really want to be saved?

CHAPTER TWENTY-SEVEN

The next morning as Laura was on her way to meet Darcy, she realized she was feeling different than she had felt in a long time. She had an excitement about the job and a sense of confusion about Alex. Still, she was starting to feel like she could breathe again. The only thing that had her so puzzled was why Alex had been acting so weird. He was so distant, not wanting to talk about anything, working late nights, and not interested in sex. She couldn't figure what could have him so distracted. He had had big projects before. What was different this time?

Suddenly a wave of fear came over Laura. Surely he wasn't having an affair.

Neither Alex nor Laura had ever been with another person, and Laura knew Alex. It just wasn't possible. She knew that having an affair was something he would never do. Right? Laura almost became panicked as she pulled into the driveway of Darcy's new residence.

By this time tears were running down her face, and she had to take a moment to compose herself. *You are making stuff up*, she told herself. *Calm down, pull it together, and get in there and do your job.*

Laura arrived at the door at ten o'clock on the dot. And right on time, Darcy opened the door to greet her with a big smile and hug. "Laura," said Darcy with lots of enthusiasm, "it is so good to see you, and I can't wait for us — I mean you — to get started on transforming this place."

Darcy was laughing when she looked up and saw a tear running from the corner of Laura's eye.

"What is it?" asked Darcy.

Laura insisted that it was nothing, but Darcy was not that naive and would not let it go.

"It can't be nothing," Darcy insisted. "Come sit down, and let's have some coffee and see what we can do to get you feeling better."

Laura and Darcy sat down on an old couch in the living room where Laura began to tell Darcy about Alex and how distant he had been lately.

Darcy wanted to assure Laura that nothing was happening, but she knew all too well what Laura was talking about. Darcy went on to say, "You don't know for sure that anything is going on, so maybe the best thing to do is just ask him." As Laura sat there with a blank stare, Darcy continued to try to encourage Laura. "Alex is a smart guy. He has a lot going for him. One of those things is his beautiful and talented wife. Why not reach out to him?"

Darcy gave Laura one more hug and gently patted her on the shoulder as Laura continued to sob.

Just then, Darcy received a text that brought a panicked look to her face. Laura immediately picked up on it. "Now it's me who should be asking what's wrong," said Laura.

"Oh, it's nothing," said Darcy. "Give me just a moment to respond to this annoying text, and then we will talk some more."

Darcy typed the text as quickly as she could. "I told you I cannot meet with you right now. My schedule is full," she typed with as much annoyance as the words indicated.

Darcy's phone binged back. "This is important. I don't think it can wait," the response read.

"We are scheduled to meet again on Monday. We can discuss it then," Darcy replied.

Another bing. Darcy was getting more frustrated by the second.

"I'm telling you we need to meet now," the text read.

With one final flurry of typing, Darcy wrote, "You will have to wait until Monday. We will talk then." She went on to type as if to drive her point home. "I'm not discussing this anymore. I'm here with my interior designer and her time is precious. Please don't text me again. I will see you Monday for our meeting."

"I'm so sorry," Darcy said to Laura, tucking her phone underneath her leg. "Now where were we?"

"I'm okay," said Laura. "Thank you for the coffee and the advice. I will think about what you said, but let's talk about something more fun — this house of yours."

Laura was excited to show Darcy the plans she had for her home, and Darcy was showing an equal amount of excitement as well.

Laura returned home around one o'clock and was starving. She immediately called for Sara and waited for her to respond.

"Hi, Mrs. Maddox. You're home," Sara said, surprised. "Did all go well?"

Laura looked at Sara with an expression she had not seen before. "First of all, Sara, I want you to call me Laura from now on. Do you think you can do that?"

Sara nodded with a grin.

"Second of all, I wanted to see if you have eaten lunch yet because I'm starving," said Laura, "and I wanted to know if you would join me for lunch."

"No," said Sara. Laura looked shocked. "That is, no, I haven't eaten," Sara said sheepishly. "I would love to join you for lunch."

Charlotte had prepared a soup and salad that looked delicious. Sara proceeded to get everything set up while Laura ran upstairs to freshen up.

"How about ten minutes, and we will meet at the table in the kitchen?" Sara suggested.

Laura responded with, "Sounds great. Let's do it."

As Laura and Sara began to dig into their salads, Laura apologized to Sara for the way she had been treating her.

Laura told Sara about things that had happened to her early on in life. She explained that guilt had a lot to do with why she acted the way she did.

"I know that is no excuse, but I have been trying for a really long time to forgive myself for something that happened a really long time ago," said Laura.

Laura went on to explain to Sara how it was not something she could easily talk about and thanked her for listening.

"Not to worry," said Sara. "You are forgiven."

Laura shifted gears and started to inquire of Sara about Alex to see if she had noticed any changes in him lately.

Sara seemed puzzled as to why Laura would be asking her, so Laura explained that she didn't mean anything bad by it. She just knew that Sara and Alex spent a good bit of time together dealing with business.

"I just want to know if he seems different to you lately," Laura said.

"What do you mean?" asked Sara.

Laura went on to explain how he had been extremely distracted lately. He couldn't focus on anything that was going on around him, she said.

Sara actually agreed with Laura. "It's funny you say that, and I know what you mean. It is like he's in outer space or just has a blank stare on his face while you are talking to him."

"Yes," Laura said. "Exactly."

Sara continued to explain how Alex was usually so attentive, but that lately when they were going over the daily agenda it was like he wasn't even in the same room with her.

As Sara and Laura continued to try to figure out what was bringing about the change, that awful feeling was creeping back up in Laura's stomach again.

"I know he has the big work project," Sara noted.

"True," said Laura, "but he has been under stress before. It is just that this time he seems so distant from everyone around here."

"It's like you said, Sara. No concentration on where he is or what he's doing," Laura continued. "He is scaring me."

Sara choked a little on her bite of food. "What do you mean scaring you?" she asked after clearing her throat. "I don't understand."

"I'm afraid there might be another woman," Laura said, amazed she was able to say the sentence out loud without sobbing.

As Laura went on pouring out her heart, she implored Sara to help shed some light on the situation.

"I really think you should talk to Alex," Sara responded. "This is really none of my business. I can't really tell you anything with certainty."

Laura pleaded with her to tell her anything, anything at all. "Tell me what you know," Laura barked in a stern voice.

With a slight hesitance at first, Sara finally told Laura about being in Alex's study recently. She was looking for some paperwork that needed to be given to Louise.

Sara assured Laura that Mr. Maddox told her it was okay to get anything she needed but not to be snoopy because there was a lot of confidential information in the office.

"Did you come across something?" asked Laura.

With another moment of hesitation, Sara took a deep breath and then told Laura about a text message she saw on Alex's phone, which had been left sitting on the desk.

Sara explained how she didn't touch the phone, but she did notice what had popped up on the screen.

"Who was it from?" asked Laura.

Sara explained that she didn't remember or recognize the name connected to the text but she did remember the contents of the text.

"It was telling him how much he was missed, and the person was considering his request that maybe they could meet after all."

As Laura broke into tears, Sara told her one more piece of information that turned her agony to anger.

"I remember at the bottom seeing four capital letters: DDIO," Sara said. "Does that mean anything to you?"

As Laura rose from the table, Sara knew the pleasantries and lunch were over.

"What does it mean?" asked Sara, knowing she might be pushing too hard.

"Please keep our conversation confidential," Laura said. "I'm going upstairs for a while. I need to think."

Sara noticed that Laura had a crazed look in her eye. That woman who a minute ago was so frightened had turned angry. Sara started to wonder if she had done the right thing. Laura went to her room and immediately texted Darcy.

The text read, "I know how busy you are, but could you give me fifteen minutes tomorrow around breakfast? I have to stop by and show you this design. I am so excited, and it simply can't wait."

Darcy knew she didn't really have the time, but she was excited as well. Darcy replied with an enthusiastic "Why not?" with a smiley face.

Darcy sent one more text. "Are you sure you want to drive all this way for just a few minutes?"

"It will be worth it," Laura replied. "Trust me. This can't wait."

Darcy replied with a thumbs up. "See you tomorrow."

CHAPTER TWENTY-EIGHT

*T*he next morning Laura took off early. She didn't have much to say to anybody, and she didn't even take the time to tell Alex goodbye. She was not in the mood for him. She would deal with him later. Right now she had other things on her mind, other people to deal with.

Letting nothing deter her, she went straight for the car, cranked the engine, and started backing out before the garage even had time to open.

She almost hit the mailbox as she flew up and out of the long winding driveway, and looking in her rearview mirror, she noticed several plants in the front yard that she had already destroyed with her tires.

She really didn't care. She had only one thing on her mind and nothing else mattered at this point.

Laura had KYCL playing on the radio, which seemed to always be running a never-ending promo about Darcy Dishes It Out. She wanted to scream. Her intensity was growing by the minute. She was becoming more and more enraged by the second. Everywhere she looked there was a reminder of Darcy. Her picture, her voice, comments about her, a billboard, a commercial, the show, Alex talking about her — she was truly everywhere.

Laura changed lanes without using a turn signal and almost ran the car in the far lane right into the barrier on the freeway.

In a total fog and letting nothing phase her, she continued toward Darcy's residence. As Laura got further down the road she continued to increase her speed and was now driving as fast as she possibly could without risking jail time.

She realized she could hardly remember the last twelve hours. She probably would have torn Alex a new one if she had seen him at all during that time. He would be a dead man, Laura thought to herself.

"Dead man!" she screamed aloud as she beat her fist on the steering wheel. Lucky for him, he didn't show up for dinner or even come to bed last night.

I'm sure he was 'working' late on the big account, she thought as a sarcastic chuckle came from her lips.

With horns honking all around her, she drove on, oblivious to anyone or anything. She wanted Darcy, and she wanted her now.

She knew she had to arrive at Darcy's no later than eight thirty. Darcy's usual staff was still maintaining her other residence, so they were splitting their time between the old and the new place.

No one would be arriving at Darcy's castle, as Laura liked to call it, until sometime around nine thirty. This was the hour of the day when Laura could get the most work done because the place was so empty and there were no interruptions. "Darcy's gonna wish for some interruptions when I get done with her," Laura said with a smirk.

Darcy told Laura she would wait on her but that she had to be on the road no later than nine. Laura arrived at Darcy's home around eight twenty-five. The somber, crying, scared demeanor that was plaguing Laura the day before was now gone. It was replaced by an intense anger and confidence she could not describe.

Laura had a complete calm on the outside but, oh, the storm that was raging down deep.

She parked the car and opened the door calmly and walked to the front door in a civilized manner. She did, however, manage to knock loud enough for the whole neighborhood to hear.

"Little pumped up there, aren't you?" said Darcy as she answered the door.

"You have no idea," said Laura.

Darcy gave Laura a hug and invited her in. Laura was calm and polite. "I'm so glad you could squeeze me in for a few minutes," said Laura.

"Well, I must admit I'm super excited about this project!" exclaimed Darcy. "Show me what you have."

"I actually have quite a bit for you," said Laura. "I have uncovered a few things since we talked last."

"Okay," said Darcy with a bit of confusion.

As Darcy and Laura walked across the foyer area it was as though Darcy was reading Laura's mind.

"Can you tell me how it's going with Alex?" Darcy asked. "I know that is a personal matter, but since you shared with me yesterday, I didn't think you would mind my asking. Are there any new developments?"

"Funny you should ask," said Laura.

"I don't follow," Darcy said with a perplexed look.

"Well, I just figured if you wanted to know anything about Alex you could have just asked him yourself, or were you just waiting until the next time you two met in person?" snarled Laura.

"I told you that everything we discussed would be confidential. I would never bring up our private conversations to Alex," insisted Darcy. "You brought these concerns to me in confidence. Laura, I would never betray your trust."

"My trust?" Laura retorted, her voice raised.

"Yes," said Darcy.

"Enough!" yelled Laura.

Darcy stood there with the most confused and terrified look on her face as Laura insisted that she should drop the act. "I know what you and my husband have been up to!" shouted Laura.

"I'm afraid I don't understand," said Darcy.

"My husband, Alex, the one you text with nonstop," retorted Laura. "The one you are always saying is so handsome and charming. Alex, the one you flirted with all night long at the Christmas party."

"I assure you that whatever you think is going on, you are wrong," said Darcy.

"I have to admit, it was genius giving me a job to throw me off the trail. Maybe this isn't your first time trying to wreck a marriage. Maybe I'm dealing with a professional. You had me so fooled."

"You don't know what you're talking about," Darcy rebutted.

"I think I do," said Laura, "and to tell you the truth, I don't think I would have believed it myself if I hadn't seen the expression on your face when he texted the other day during our conversation."

Darcy tried to explain to Laura that she had it wrong. The look of concern on her face had nothing to do with Alex or his firm.

"I was anxious," said Darcy. "That was my agent, and I'm in the middle of a contract renewal that's driving me crazy."

Laura called Darcy a liar and pushed her hard enough that she stumbled backward across the foyer, hitting her shoulder against the wall and losing her footing.

Darcy turned back to face Laura and slowly tried to scoot away from her. Laura dropped to her knees and screamed, "Whhhhhyyyyyy?" and slapped Darcy in the face.

As Darcy struggled to stand on wobbly legs, she pleaded with Laura. "I don't know what you think you know, but you are wrong."

Laura lunged at Darcy as Darcy screamed, "You need to leave now!"

But Laura swung her fist, punching Darcy in the side of her face.

"Stop it, Laura," Darcy said.

"Not happening," Laura growled as her aggression ramped up and she threw another punch, this time laying Darcy out.

As Darcy's head hit the floor, Laura jumped up and pulled back her leg in an effort to kick Darcy in the stomach. Darcy, out of pure instinct, pushed forward, catching Laura's leg and knocking her back.

Laura stumbled, and Darcy gave her another shove to push her away, not realizing how close she was to the edge of the stairs.

Laura fell backward, her head slamming against the bottom of the stone marble staircase. Blood began pouring from the back of Laura's head as her body lay limp with her neck distorted and eyes gazing.

Darcy looked on in horror while only inches away, Laura's lifeless body was lying in a pool of her own blood.

Darcy quickly scurried away from the stairs on her hands and knees as she was gasping for breath following the confrontation.

Darcy immediately pulled her phone from her vest pocket and dialed 911. Barely able to speak, she gave her address and said there had been an accident and that she needed both police and paramedics immediately.

By the time the police and paramedics arrived, there was nothing to be done.

Laura was dead on arrival, and Darcy was in disbelief at the events that had taken place over the last few minutes.

CHAPTER TWENTY-NINE

*I*t was approximately ten thirty in the morning when Alex's secretary buzzed him on line two of his office phone. "Mr. Maddox, there is a man on line one for you."

"I'm going to need you to take a message, Mary. I'm in the middle of something important right now," Alex said.

Less than a minute later, Mary buzzed back and explained how the man stressed the call was urgent and that he needed to speak to him right away.

Alex insisted that he could not speak to the man at that time, but then Mary told him it was about Laura. Alex's feeling of frustration quickly halted, and his emotions turned to concern as he answered line two.

"This is Alex Maddox," he said.

"Mr. Maddox, my name is Deputy Scott," said the voice on the other end of the line. Deputy Scott continued to explain to Alex that his wife had been involved in an accident.

"Where is she?" Alex asked with a trembling voice.

"We are currently at the residence of Darcy Campbell. Do you know the address? … Mr. Maddox, Mr. Maddox, are you there?"

Alex dropped the phone before he could even answer Deputy Scott's question.

As Alex grabbed his jacket, he did a quick mental check to make sure he had everything he needed — keys, cell phone, wallet. Alex blew past Mary without so much as a whisper and wasted no time on waiting for the elevator.

Alex descended the stairway three and four steps at a time, slinging open the door at the bottom of the stairs and heading full speed for the car.

Alex was buckling his seatbelt and adjusting the mirrors as he took off for the interstate.

Alex knew it was bad, but he did not realize how bad it could be until he arrived on the scene. As Alex wove his way toward Darcy's house, there was a large scene of emergency vehicles, including police cars, fire trucks, and ambulances.

Alex's heart was sinking farther and farther into his stomach as he did his best to explain to the officer guarding the scene who he was and why he needed to get inside the home.

Still trying his hardest to push his way past security, the officers were holding Alex on the spot until a frantic voice called from the steps.

"Let him through!" It was a shaking Darcy who was yelling to the officers.

They released Alex, and he headed toward Darcy.

"I got here as soon as I could," said Alex. "What's going on? What happened?"

"You don't know?" Darcy asked in exasperation.

"Know what?" Alex asked, confused. "You're scaring me."

Darcy grabbed Alex by the arm and dragged him through the front door where she pointed Alex's gaze toward the blood stains on the floor.

"I don't understand," said Alex. "Where is Laura? They said there was an accident involving my wife. Where is she?"

Darcy — in the slowest of motion — pointed to a gurney that was sitting on the left side of the room with two police officers and a coroner standing over it.

"It's not possible," said Alex as he fell to his knees. "I don't understand. They said there was an accident, not that she was, was …."

Alex became silent, realizing he couldn't bring himself to say the word. Alex mustered the strength to stand and began to wobble, as if he were drunk, toward Laura's body. Darcy reached out her hands to Alex's shoulders to steady him.

Just then a voice came from behind Alex. It was Detective Scott. "Mr. Maddox, I'm sorry to ask you this, but we need to show you the body for identification." Alex looked at him with the blankest of stares.

"Do you think you can do this?" asked Detective Scott.

Alex once again looked at him with disbelief and nodded his head in a yes motion.

Alex and the officer walked over to the gurney where Detective Scott asked the coroner to unzip the bag.

Alex fell to his knees, yelling Laura's name and crying hysterically. Darcy stood on the other side of the room, still in disbelief at what had happened.

About that time, another officer asked Darcy if she would like to go ahead and give her statement, and she said she would try.

The officer escorted Darcy to the other room where Darcy gave an account of the events that had taken place in the last few hours. Darcy explained everything from the moment she and Laura had agreed to meet until that terrible moment when she was looking down at Laura's body and calling 911 for help.

When Darcy had finished her statement and was released by the officer, she walked back into the main room to see Alex sitting at the bottom of the staircase with a stare of pure nothingness. It was as if he wasn't even present in his body.

Darcy went over and sat down next to him, but nothing was said for a couple of minutes. Then Alex broke the silence with the statement he had already said so many times. "I don't understand. How could this have happened? It makes no sense."

Darcy suggested that they move into the other room and let the police and paramedics continue their jobs.

Once they had settled into the living room, Alex looked at Darcy and said, "Can you tell me what happened?"

Darcy hesitantly began to talk about the events of the morning and explained to him what Laura was accusing her of and how the conversation escalated until Laura began to physically attack her.

"So you pushed her into the stairs?" said Alex, realizing immediately how insensitive that sounded.

"I had no intention of pushing her into the stairs or even hurting her. I just needed to get away long enough to call for help," Darcy said.

"I can't believe it came to this," said Alex. "This is all our fault. You and me. The Bible says the wages of sin is death. This is our fault."

"What do you mean, 'our fault'?" asked Darcy.

"You know what I mean," said Alex.

Darcy insisted that she had no idea what Alex meant. Darcy also demanded to know why Laura thought they were having some sort of affair.

"You know why, Darcy. You know exactly why," insisted Alex. "What I don't know is how she found out."

"Found out what?" Darcy said with a look of utter dismay on her face.

"Are you sure you want to discuss this here?" asked Alex.

"What are you talking about?" Darcy demanded in a voice of both frustration and anger.

"Us, Darcy. I'm talking about us," Alex barked back at her.

"You mean the building, our work project? The business meetings? What are you talking about, Alex?" Darcy persisted.

"No, not the building, not the business meetings," Alex said with frustration. "She must have found out about us."

"Alex, for the last time, what are you talking about?" Darcy asked again as she stood there with a puzzled look on her face.

"You're in denial," said Alex. "I need to know, where does this leave us?"

"Are you really thinking about the job at a time like this?" Darcy said with disgust.

"No, Darcy," Alex said, then turned away realizing how loud he was. "No, Darcy," he repeatedly quietly. "Where does this leave us?"

"Alex, you're scaring me," Darcy said. "Why did Laura think there was something going on between us?"

"Because of the texts," Alex said. "She must have found out about the texts."

"What texts, Alex?" Darcy was really confused now.

"What do you mean, 'What texts?'" Alex asked. "All of them. All of our conversations. Everything we were planning to do. All of the pictures you sent me. All of the intimate things we have shared for nearly two months now. Laura must have found out."

Darcy explained to Alex that Laura told her in confidence that she suspected him of having some sort of affair or correspondence with someone. "I just never dreamed she would determine it was with me. Why would she think it was me?"

"Because it was you," said Alex.

Darcy looked at him with an expression of total confusion. Never in her life had she been as confused and scared as she was right now.

"I don't understand, Alex. I have never talked with you outside of business or the Christmas party."

"What about the note, Darcy?" Alex asked. "The note in the envelope. The one that you gave Sara at the Christmas party to give to me."

"What are you talking about?" Darcy said forcefully.

Alex reached into his jacket pocket and pulled out a piece of paper and showed her the note that she had left for him. He handed it to Darcy and let her read it.

"Alex, this is not my writing. This is not my number. And this is not something I would do. This is not me. Do you understand? This is not me."

"It is you," Alex said. He showed her all of the many texts they had shared, along with so many pictures.

As Darcy scrolled through all of the conversations and looked at the photographs on the phone, she could barely keep herself from throwing up.

"Where did you get these, Alex, and who has been writing all this stuff?" asked Darcy.

"What do mean?" Alex asked through tears.

"Who could be on the other end of these texts, Alex?" asked Darcy.

"I thought you were," said Alex. "I thought you were."

As Darcy handed the phone back to Alex, she couldn't think of words to convey what she was feeling.

"It's not me, Alex," she said. "I never want to see your face again. You're fired. I'll be contacting The Landing to get a new account manager, but I never want to see your face or hear your voice ever again."

Alex felt even more lonely and distraught than he had a few moments earlier. In a defeated and saddened voice, Alex agreed with Darcy. "Last thing," he said. "If it wasn't you all this time, then who did this to me?"

"You did it to yourself, Alex. You made this choice. Now go home. Your son is going to need you. He just lost his mother," Darcy said with a look that could cut through steel.

As Alex started to leave, Darcy said, "One more thing. If I were you, I might consider getting a new house manager."

CHAPTER THIRTY

*A*lex was experiencing a roller coaster of emotions as he drove home. One minute he was filled with grief, the next it was guilt, and the next it was anger. He was beating his emotions to death. And he knew he deserved it.

Tears were running down his face as he called in to the office to let them know he would not be returning for the day.

While sitting at the red light before entering the freeway, Alex's cries and screams were so violent and loud he was sure they could be heard for miles away. He couldn't believe the events of the day and everything that had unfolded over the last few weeks and months.

How could he have been so blinded and selfish? He knew how wrong he was and how he had let evil deceive him.

There was no justification for what he had done and the way he had been acting, but why did he have to pay such a high price for his sin?

If not for Ben, he might have been willing to drive into the upcoming telephone pole at top speed. He knew what he was about to face in the weeks to come. While the loss of Laura was the most devastating of all, Alex knew there was much more devastation to come.

The loss of the account. Possibly his job. His reputation. The humiliation he would bring upon his family. All those things were bad, but they were small in comparison to the idea that Laura died not trusting him. How would he tell their parents?

Alex began to think about how he was going to be able to live with this. Could there ever be any forgiveness?

With all these emotions and all of his suffering, he knew the pain of the day was just beginning. Alex was about to have the confrontation of a lifetime with Sara. He knew what was coming, and it was not going to be gentle. So many questions were running through his mind, but the biggest one of all was "Why?"

Alex walked in the door with a look that Sara had never seen before. It was blank and cold but angry.

"Mr. Maddox, you're home early," Sara said innocently. Sara immediately made eye contact with Alex and added, "What can I do to help you, Alex? You look stressed."

Alex asked Sara to join him in his study.

"Gladly," she said in a cheerful voice. "I just need a few minutes to get the staff settled and then I'll be right in."

"It wasn't a request," Alex barked. "My study, now!"

Sara walked timidly toward the study while the rest of the staff continued with their daily routine.

Stella and Maggie had just finished cleaning the study and could sense the tension in the room as they were on their way out the door. As Sara stepped inside the study, Alex, in the calmest voice he could muster, asked Sara to please close the door.

Sara stood just inside the door and several feet away from the desk, but Alex insisted she have a seat in front of the desk. She stared at him hesitantly as she walked toward the chair and lowered herself down into the seat ever so slowly.

"What is this all about?" she asked, her face showing a look of confusion as Alex sat down in the chair next to her. Alex took out the note from the night of the Christmas party and threw it on her lap.

"You want to tell me about this?" asked Alex, trying not to let his voice tremble. Before Sara could say a word, Alex followed up with, "Since we have been texting so openly for many weeks now, why don't you just tell me the truth?"

Sara stared at him as if she had no idea what he was talking about.

"There is nothing you can say or do to push me any lower than I am right now," Alex said. "I need the truth. What is going on?"

"It's not what you think," Sara responded. "When I interviewed with you, I felt a connection. I feel like I have always had a connection with you from the moment we met. There is something different about you, Alex. Something special. Something Laura never really appreciated."

Alex wanted to slap her in the face as she continued to talk, but he restrained himself.

"Don't you see, Alex? You and I are connected," Sara continued. "I did it for us. My job was to protect and help you. You, Alex. We don't need Laura here to make this a family."

With Alex just sitting and listening, Sara continued to talk.

"She will be fine financially. She will land on her feet," Sara said. "But she is not the right person for you."

Alex looked up from his gaze, tears now trickling from his eyes.

"Alex, you can be so much more," Sara pleaded. "Divorce her and let me be with you so you can finally have the woman you deserve."

Sara reached over to take Alex's hand as if everything she was saying was normal and he should be in total agreement with her.

"I can't divorce her!" yelled Alex.

"You can," encouraged Sara. "You just have to do it."

"I can't!" yelled Alex.

The rest of the staff was beginning to draw near to the door as they could hear the confrontation from the other side.

"You're just scared," said Sara.

Alex stood with such force it threw his chair about five feet across the room.

"She's dead, Sara! Do you hear me? Laura is dead!" screamed Alex.

"What do mean, 'dead'?" Sara gasped. "I don't understand."

Alex went on to explain that she confronted Darcy, the real Darcy, about all the texts she had been sending him. He explained how Laura attacked Darcy that morning in her home and there was a scuffle. He told her about Laura crashing into the stairs.

"She broke her neck," said Alex. "Severe brain trauma. She died instantly." By this time, Alex was sobbing as the words came out of his mouth.

Sara moved in to hug Alex to comfort him. For half a second Alex forgot himself and started to hug her back. But in a flash Alex pushed her away.

"Are you crazy? This is not a game. My wife who I love is dead."

"If you loved her so much then why did you cheat on her?" Sara asked with absolutely no compassion or remorse.

"I didn't cheat on her," insisted Alex.

"There is more than one kind of cheating, and you know it. Besides, she wasn't supposed to die. She was just supposed to leave," Sara said as Alex looked at her in horror.

"I don't think you're getting it, Alex. My point is, if you loved her so much, you would not have spent hours and hours talking with me over the past few months.

"You're right, Alex. It was me. You love me and I have the texts to prove it."

Sara pulled out her phone and scrolled through the record of everything they had texted about over the last few months, reading parts and pieces of the text aloud for Alex.

"You love me and I love you. I did this for you. I did it for us," Sara said with a most sincere look. "Everything you said in your texts about wanting to be together is now possible."

"Did you show Laura the texts?" Alex asked.

"I didn't have to," Sara said. "She could tell how distant you were becoming and the obvious lack of physical affection was a big hint as well."

Alex fell back onto the desk as Sara continued to speak her mind.

"It's not like it was a big secret what you were doing. The whole staff was talking about it."

"Did you tell her?" Alex asked again.

"I just pointed her in the right direction," Sara said. "She did the rest. She's crazy, you know. Always has been."

As Alex started toward Sara, Sara continued to speak. "She was mean to me from the moment I met her, and she didn't even have a reason. Who treats someone like that?"

"I want you to gather your belongings and get out of my home and my life!" Alex screamed.

"You don't mean that," said Sara.

"You are fired," said Alex. "And I never want to see you again."

"You don't mean that," said Sara, gently rubbing Alex on the shoulder.

Alex grabbed her by the arm and pulled her toward the door. "I want you out of my house now!"

"Think about what you're doing," Sara said.

"If you don't leave now, I will bring you up on charges of manslaughter. And you know I have the means to do it," Alex threatened.

"Fine, I'm going," said Sara, "but you love me and I love you, Alex. I have from the moment I met you."

With those final words, Sara walked out of the study, making eye contact with each of the staff members as if to wish them well. She then stepped out the door toward the guest house.

Alex was emotionally drained but was thankful he would never lay eyes on that evil woman ever again.

CHAPTER THIRTY-ONE

*T*he air outside was brisk with a cool breeze blowing. The sun was shining brightly on this beautiful Saturday morning, and Sara couldn't wait to get going on her morning exercise.

It was the last day of February, and the past few days seemed like a blur.

Sara was always up bright and early to get her morning run in. It was something she never liked to miss.

She left her basement apartment around eight o'clock as usual, knowing that it would give her plenty of time to do the three-mile course before returning home. Sara was walking and cooling down as she approached the house around eight forty-five.

Rita and Fred were sitting on the front porch swing sipping their coffee without a care in the world. They were always there to greet Sara as she returned from her run.

Wiping the sweat from her forehead, Sara walked up to the porch with a big smile on her face. She always loved seeing Fred and Rita.

Fred greeted her with a friendly wave as Rita stood up to hug Sara.

Sara always thought the sweat and smell would deter Rita, but she never missed the opportunity to give her a hug and tell her how much she loved her.

"How is my sweet girl doing today?" asked Rita.

"I'm really good," said Sara. "I want to thank you again for letting me back into the basement apartment."

"Think nothing of it," said Rita as Fred gave a little grunt.

"Love you, too," said Sara as she blew a kiss to Fred. "I'm sorry I ruined your man cave right before March Madness."

"Nonsense," insisted Rita. "You know you are welcome to stay here as long as you like. That grumpy old man will be just fine," Rita said with a laugh as she pointed to Fred.

"I appreciate it," said Sara. "I love you guys so much."

"We love you too, Sara," said Fred with a smirk.

"I do have some leads on a new job," said Sara. "I'm not sure how long I'll be here, but I will get back on my feet soon."

Rita assured her she would find something soon, and in the meantime she should just enjoy the apartment.

"I'm going to head in and get a shower and grab a cup of coffee," said Sara.

She blew Rita and Fred one last kiss as she headed toward the basement apartment to get ready for the day.

As Sara reached her apartment, it was around eight fifty-five. She had just enough time to get her coffee and settle in for her weekly Saturday appointment.

It was nine o'clock and Sara was mesmerized by the writing on the front of her journal. Sara Christine Ponders, she read aloud.

She was thinking how funny it was that everyone called her Chris for so long. Sara was a much prettier name in her opinion.

Opening her journal, she picked up the pen and began to write.

Saturday, 9:00 a.m., February 29 — Week 9

It has been a little more than a week now since I was asked to leave my job at the Maddox residence. It is hard to believe all that has transpired in the last two months.

I know that I will never have the chance to be with Alex, and for that matter, probably never even talk to him again, but I did accomplish my goal.

I always knew he could do better than Laura, and at least now he is not married to her anymore. How did someone as kind and loving as Alex ever fall for someone as mean and ugly as Laura? It just made no sense.

I know I am doing the right thing. I remember how satisfying it was to take down the first member of Triple Threat and how that motivated me.

I have now managed to take down two members of Triple Threat, and it has brought me even more satisfaction.

The plan took a little detour, but I would still consider it a success. I can't wait to see how good it is going to feel to take down all three. I can hardly even contain myself at the thought of ending them for good. It has been a long time coming.

Next stop, San Antonio, and soon there will be no more Triple Threat.

It's 10:00 a.m. Until next week.

CHAPTER THIRTY-TWO

*A*lex had used every bit of strength he had in him to survive the past few weeks. A lot of time in prayer and Baby Ben were the only things keeping him going. He had many layers of grief to work through and the local pastor suggested starting with finding a way to forgive himself as well as Sara.

He knew the pitch all too well. Jesus died on the cross to forgive our sins and all we have to do is accept the free gift of His grace to be forgiven and have eternal life in heaven with Him. It's not that Alex didn't believe. He did. In fact, he knew God's promise of redemption is the only reason he forgave himself back in high school and how he knew he would be able to find his way to forgiveness again. But that didn't mean it would be easy. The guilt and shame weighed so heavily on him.

And now this — how could this be happening now? — Alex thought as he stared at the floor in disbelief.

It had only been five weeks since the death of Laura, and now here he was on a Wednesday morning in San Antonio sitting on the front row dressed in black again — this time to say goodbye to Michelle.

Alex had to be there for Trevor. He had been his best friend since before he could remember. Trevor was devastated to say the least. Alex knew all too well the path Trevor and the kids were about to have to walk.

It was as if life was playing some kind of a sick joke on Alex. Either taking or destroying everyone and everything he loved piece by piece.

Alex already had too much to bear, and now he would have to hold Trevor up as well.

The official report was that Michelle was run off the road by a drunk driver. It was a one-car accident that happened late the previous Thursday night. The autopsy revealed Michelle was killed on impact when she hit the tree.

As a few members of the local Baptist church sang "Amazing Grace," Alex continued to let his mind wander in a state of confusion at all that had happened.

First Crystal, then Laura, and now Michelle. It almost seemed too crazy to be a coincidence, and Alex was beginning to wonder.

Alex was one of the pallbearers along with two guys he knew from high school and several of Michelle's cousins.

The service in the church was short and followed by a small graveside service to say a final goodbye. Alex sat with Michelle's parents, the children, and Trevor.

After the service, a smaller group close to the family headed to the house for a time of visitation.

Alex knew Trevor could have done without that, but it was part of the process and he wasn't going to argue.

After the last of the close friends and family left for the night, Trevor and Alex finally had a chance to talk. Alex decided he would stick around for a day or two before heading back home. Grace and the rest of the household staff were taking good care of Ben, and Alex really felt like Trevor could use him right now.

It was the most mellow and somber the two of them had ever been in their entire lives. Neither one was interested in getting in trouble or making a joke; they were both just completely broken and sad.

Early Friday morning, Alex was sitting watching the news as Trevor slept. The anchor was rattling on, but Alex could care less about what was going on in the world. He popped out of his haze when his phone rang. He did not recognize the number and usually would just ignore the call, but for some reason he answered. He figured it was a sales call of some kind. He figured he would just listen to this poor soul try to sell him something before hanging up on him.

"Hello," said Alex.

"Hello, sir. I am wanting to get in touch with Alex Maddox, please."

"You got him," said Alex, expecting the man on the other end to go straight into some type of sales pitch.

The voice on the other end of the phone introduced himself as Mr. Barnes. He explained that he had an application with him from one of Alex's former employees. He wanted to know if Alex would take a few minutes and answer some questions. He explained that she had Alex listed as her top reference for a job.

Alex perked up a little. He actually welcomed the distraction, if only for a few minutes. Besides, he had nothing better to do for the time being.

Alex started by asking the man the name of the employee.

"Her name is Sara Ponders," said Mr. Barnes.

"I'm sorry," said Alex in a bit of a shaky voice. "I never had anyone in my employment by that name."

Mr. Barnes replied, "Well, I do see here that Ponders is her maiden name."

Mr. Barnes looked through the file a bit more and then said, "Oh yes, she said she prefers to go by Ponders now that she is no longer married, but you might have known her as Sara Patterson."

Just then an awful chill came over Alex as he said, "You will have to call me back."

Sara Patterson, Sara Ponders …. Could it be?

He hung up the phone and called out to Trevor. Even with all the yelling and racket Alex was making, Trevor never even stirred from his sleep.

Alex burst into Trevor's room and shook him awake, asking, "Where is your senior yearbook?"

A frustrated Trevor said, "What are you talking about?" as he rolled over to fall back asleep.

"Trevor, where is your senior yearbook?" Alex asked frantically. Trevor groaned. "Our senior yearbook, where is it? Do you have it?" asked Alex with some authority.

"On the bookshelf next to the T.V.," said Trevor, still half asleep.

Alex grabbed the yearbook and headed back to the living room couch at a desperate pace.

As Alex flipped the pages, he almost fainted when he looked down on page thirty-four and saw there in black and white, the picture of the girl who had committed suicide so long ago.

Sara Christine Ponders. "Chris didn't die," Alex whispered to himself. "She didn't die."

Alex was trying his best to wrap his head around all that he had just discovered.

He was marking on a notepad everything he knew and trying to put the pieces of this puzzle together.

By the time Trevor stumbled out of bed an hour later, Alex realized all that had happened and knew that his theory about it not being a coincidence was right. The deaths of Laura, Crystal, and Michelle were no accident. They were planned.

It took Alex the rest of the day to explain it all to Trevor and help him connect the dots. They both fell asleep that Friday night emotionally and mentally whipped.

Saturday morning at nine o'clock as Alex was sitting in Trevor's living room in San Antonio, sipping on coffee and still trying to wrap his mind around all that had happened, the doorbell rang. Alex went to answer the door, and there stood a UPS delivery man holding a package.

"Are you Alex?" the delivery man asked.

"Yes," Alex said.

The delivery man explained the instructions that came with the package, and that it was to be delivered at nine o'clock a.m. and that Alex was to open it right away.

Alex was both confused and frightened as he sat down on the couch to open the package. Meanwhile, 1,783 miles away, Sara was sitting in the middle of the gymnasium at Heights Central. As Alex looked inside the package, he pulled out a disposable cell phone with instructions to call the number attached to the phone.

"Hello, Alex," a familiar voice said. "Do you know who this is?"

"Yes," said Alex.

"Do you see the envelope in the bottom of the package?" asked Sara.

Alex did not respond as Sara made one final statement.

"Make sure you open it."

Just then a single gunshot rang out in the gymnasium of their old high school. As Sara's body lay there on the cold gym floor, so did the 1851 Colt Navy Revolver that Alex so treasured from his Grandpa.

Alex dropped the phone and immediately opened the package, where he saw a Polaroid print of Crystal, Michelle, and Laura.

Written across the bottom were three words.

"NOW IT'S OVER."

EPILOGUE

*A*lex changed his return flight from San Antonio to Salt Lake City to make an unexpected trip to New York City. The flight landed in time for him to pick up the rental car and circle by Laura's parents' home for a quick visit before heading to stay with his parents for the night.

The next morning as Alex drove toward Principal Saunders' home just outside the city, an overwhelming amount of confusion pressed on his heart and mind.

As Alex parked the car, he could see the old man sitting and drinking his coffee in the front porch swing.

Alex took just a minute to gather his thoughts as he turned off the engine and unbuckled his seatbelt.

Alex exited the car and slowly started to head toward the front porch.

As he walked up the steps, he made his way to the seat across from the porch swing.

Principal Saunders barely even looked up at Alex and finally broke the silence when he said, "I know you have some questions. And you deserve some answers."

Alex really only had one question and was hoping to get a straight answer.

"Why did you tell us Christine Ponders had died?"

Principal Saunders was remembering the conversation he had with Ms. Willis, the school counselor, as they were leaving the hospital that day, like it was yesterday.

It had been so long ago and yet it was as fresh a memory as what he had eaten for breakfast.

As Principal Saunders started to answer Alex's question, his eyes started to get red and teary.

He said, "There was no excuse for what I told you that day. I was outraged at what had happened. My judgment was clouded, and I made a terrible decision."

Principal Saunders went on to explain that Ms. Willis' daughter had attempted suicide when she was a teenager. He explained that it had happened before she had taken the job at Heights Central.

"She wanted anyone who had anything to do with Christine's situation to know what an awful thing they had done." said Principal Saunders.

"Ms. Willis convinced me that telling you kids that someone had overdosed would not make enough of an impact."

Principal Saunders shared how he was hesitant at first, but he eventually came to agree with Ms. Willis that the students needed to understand the importance of not treating others badly.

"It was one lie," said Principal Saunders. "It was supposed to serve a greater purpose."

"Christine and her aunt were moving away when she healed. They wanted no contact with the school from that point forward. It was a perfect story. Who would ever know?"

Principal Saunders was shaking his head even now at the very words coming out of his mouth.

Alex sat there in silence rocking back and forth in the chair as Principal Saunders continued. "I just remember telling myself it was one lie. How much harm could it do? How much harm could it really do?"

As the question hung heavy in the air, Alex looked down at his well-worn key ring, stood up and snickered as he showed the inscribed Scripture to Principal Saunders. Luke 8:17. "What does it mean?"

"It means that God knows what He is talking about," Alex said in a humble voice as he turned away and headed toward the car.

For nothing is secret that will not be revealed, nor anything hidden that will not be known and come to light. Luke 8:17

ABOUT THE AUTHOR

Jason B. Rash

Jason B. Rash knew he would one day publish a dramatic fictional story, even though his background is in physical education and sports activities. When he decided to go for it with this first book, the story he created almost wrote itself. Jason spends his days keeping swimmers safe and enjoys competitive pickleball on the side. He and his wife, Jennifer, call Birmingham, Alabama, home.

Made in the USA
Columbia, SC
28 March 2022

58246789R00100